Child Support

DATE		
JUL 1 0 1999		
SEP 0 8 1999		
FEB 0 7 2000		
MAR 1 4 2000		

H ugh
C ent

 W9-BZV-031

Child Support Survival Guide

How to Get Results Through Child Support Enforcement Agencies

By
Bonnie M. White
and
Douglas Pipes

CAREER PRESS
3 Tice Road, P.O. Box 687
Franklin Lakes, NJ 07417
1-800-CAREER-1
201-848-0310 (NJ and outside U.S.)
Fax: 201-848-1727

CHILD SUPPORT SURVIVAL GUIDE
HOW TO GET RESULTS THROUGH CHILD SUPPORT
ENFORCEMENT AGENCIES
ISBN 1-56414-310-4 $12.99
Cover design by Hub Graphics Corp.
Printed in the U.S.A. by Book-mart Press

To order this title by mail, please include price as noted above, $2.50 handling per order, and $1.50 for each book ordered. Send to: Career Press, Inc., 3 Tice Road, P.O. Box 687, Franklin Lakes, NJ 07417.

Or call toll-free 1-800-CAREER-1 (NJ and Canada: 201-848-0310) to order using VISA or MasterCard, or for further information on books from Career Press.

Library of Congress Cataloging-in-Publication Data

White, Bonnie M., 1955-
    Child support survival guide : how to get results through child
support enforcement agencies / by Bonnie M. White and Douglas Pipes.
    P.   Cm.
    Includes index.
    ISBN 1-56414-310-4 (pbk.)
    1. Child support--Government policy--United States. 2. Desertion
and non-support--Government policy--United States.   3. Custody of
children--Economic aspects--United States.   I. Pipes, Douglas,
1943-   II. Title.
    HV741.W398   1997
346.7301'72--dc21   97-36690
                                                                          CIP

Dedication

This book is dedicated to child support enforcement workers everywhere. Without your hard work and commitment to this cause, our children could not prosper.

....
Acknowledgments

Writers who specialize in a particular field often need the support of peers and the assistance of friends and relatives to produce a book that is the first of its kind. This book is no exception. A great many people assisted us throughout the long research, writing, and publishing process.

We extend our thanks to Gary Yancey, Tom Torlakson, Gayle Graham, Wayne Doss, Daryll Grubbs, Pam Franko, and Dan Barnes, who provided this behind-the-scenes support.

We are also grateful to Betsy Mattheson of the Office of Child Support Enforcement; to Bruce Kaspari and Allenya Kirby of the California Department of Justice Parent Locator Service for their assistance in obtaining current information and in providing editorial suggestions; and to Sharon Ruddick from B. Dalton Books, where the idea for this book began.

Moral support accolades to Monica Perkins, Shiela Honey, and Lori Moore who encouraged us from beginning to end, and to Jill Brauner for suggesting the title for the book and for helping when the computer crashed.

We thank our families who encouraged us and put up with our long hours and erratic schedules. They are Bonnie's parents, Manuel and Beverly Ramos; Bonnie's children, Eric and Christina; and Doug's wife, Diane.

And finally, much thanks to our literary agent, Doris Michaels, who believed in this project and knew a good thing when she saw it, and to our publisher, Ron Fry at Career Press, who took a chance on broaching a subject never before published for the general public.

Contents

Why You Need This Book

Do you have problems getting the child support payments that are due your children? You are not alone; more than 40 million parents in this country struggle with problems relating to child support.

Perhaps you are a divorced mother of two children, your husband has left town, has fallen behind in his child support payments, and has dropped the medical insurance coverage for your children. You have repeatedly taken him to court over these matters. In the process, you have paid attorney fees and court costs, and you have missed work and lost income. All to no avail.

Or you might be a divorced father who has fallen behind on child support payments. You are now suffering the legal consequences of divorce that have left you in financial ruin. Or you might just have been served with a summons and complaint that names you as the father of a child, and you doubt whether you are really that child's parent.

If you are involved in a child support legal action, problems crop up that can confuse you and complicate your life and your children's lives. When you are faced with a problem in you child support case, do you know what to do about that problem?

Child support is a highly charged emotional issue for everyone involved and child support disputes can have long-term financial consequences that can be disastrous if they aren't handled properly. Fighting courtroom battles over child support can also be as much of an emotional drain as it can be a financial drain. Bank accounts dwindle when child support confrontations increase, and in the end, the children are the real losers. Children do not understand why their parents don't speak to each other anymore or why they can't have a new bicycle or new school clothes. Children are usually aware that when their parents do speak to each other, tempers flair, feelings are hurt, and life styles are forever changed for everyone in the family.

Child support laws are complex. Enforcement of these laws can be so time-consuming and expensive that most people are unable to handle child support disputes on their own. When faced with a severe shortage of available information about a child support system that creates so much confusion, many people do not learn about the resources that are available to assist them in child support-related problems. For many people, hiring an attorney to represent them or a private investigator to assist them are options that are out of their financial reach. Some low-cost consumer groups and legal aid clinics can assist low-income parents in establishing a child support order. But enforcing a child support order successfully is beyond the reach of the average person.

Child Support Enforcement (CSE) agencies are far and away the most affordable available resource to help parents who are embroiled in child support problems. The services offered by CSE agencies are provided at little or no cost to the parents. CSE agencies—their functions, policies, procedures, and limitations—are the focus of this book.

Federal and state laws that regulate child support, paternity, and child support enforcement enable the CSE agency to assist parents in resolving their child support matters by acting as an impartial third party. But in order for you to have your child support case managed effectively by a CSE agency, you must know how these agencies operate. You must know your rights in the child support process, and you must know how to assist the CSE agency in resolving your child support problems. The best way to get results through CSE agencies is for you to become aware of the laws governing child support, to become knowledgeable about the procedures used by CSE agencies, to know what CSE agencies can and cannot do for and to you, and to know your rights in this system. By becoming educated about the child support enforcement process, you can greatly improve the chances that you will achieve your desired result: providing for your children while keeping your financial livelihood intact.

This book is the first comprehensive guide on Child Support Enforcement (CSE) agencies written for custodial and noncustodial parents. It provides the information both parties need to maneuver their ways through a complicated system. For years people have been uninformed when dealing with CSE agencies. The crux of the matter is that most custodial parents and noncustodial parents do not know how this system works, how it can affect them, and what rights they have in this system.

The CSE agency performs vital services, including establishing paternity, establishing child support orders, and enforcing child support and spousal support orders. CSE agencies are regulated and funded by the federal government. The CSE agency is legally responsible for ensuring that all children whose cases they handle receive the financial support they need from both parents. CSE agencies can locate missing parents, implement severe enforcement actions on non-payers, monitor and track child support payments, and modify existing court orders. CSE agencies work to remove dependent families from the welfare rolls by collecting regular child support payments for these children.

However, whether you are the custodial parent or the noncustodial parent, dealing with this government agency can be a frustrating experience. If this is how you feel, take heart, because much of your frustration might be needless. It may be caused only by your lack of knowledge on how the CSE system works. Knowledge is power and this book arms you with the knowledge you'll need to work effectively in the system.

Stumbling through the CSE system is a journey no one wants to take. It is an odyssey that begins with the end of a relationship that may have lasted many years or just one night. But if you have decided to read this book, the outcome of this relationship for you has been the same regardless of the history of the relationship: You have a child or children who need to be supported. Partners who were once in love with each other and who were prepared to spend the rest of their lives together now find themselves dealing with the emotional issues that come from a broken relationship. As reality sets in, they realize their financial livelihoods are now in danger. In a perfect world, both parents would be happy with the arrangements for supporting their children even after their relationship is over. But then, in a perfect world parents would not separate. The CSE system was established to help rectify some of the damage caused by these breakups.

The words *child support* can ignite anger and hostility in even the most amicable of relationships. Often, both parents are angry with each other when their relationship ends. While some former partners are amicable at the onset of the breakup of their relationship, their mutual love for their children is often overridden by monetary disputes. Either you are the parent who needs support for your children, or you are the parent responsible for paying it. No matter how you slice it, child support issues are likely to become a central part of your post-separation relationship.

What is a paternity issue? How do I go about getting a child support order when I can't afford an attorney? How do you make the other parent pay? How long will this process take? What gives you the right to attach my wages? Do I need an attorney? Isn't there some way to get action on my case? How do I reach someone through your telephone system? How does a parent get answers to these questions? How does a parent get action on his or her case? In this book, we answer these frequently asked questions, guide you through the child support enforcement system, and explain the rights and responsibilities you will have in the system.

You may be surprised to find that you *do not* need an attorney to represent you on child support issues. Attorneys charge you to answer your questions. Some encourage the noncustodial parent to fight the CSE agency in court; the attorney is then retained for a fee. The end result is often that the noncustodial parent ends up paying the same amount of child support that the CSE office advised should have been paid long before the courtroom battle took place. In those situations, not only does the noncustodial parent pay child support, but that parent must also pay the additional cost of attorneys' fees.

Some custodial parents pay thousands of dollars on their own to obtain a support order, then find they are unable to locate the noncustodial parent, or they are unable to enforce the order. By the time these parents turn to a CSE agency for help, they are often owed thousands of dollars in back child support.

The federal government has mandated that all states become fully automated in child support functions or risk a reduction in the federal funding for child support enforcement. Most states are presently developing their automated systems. As an example, California's statewide computer system is still in its early implementation stages. The plan is for every county's CSE agency to be linked to this automated system. The system will simplify and automate many tasks, but the system has taken years to develop and may not become fully operational for several more years. Many states are already online with their own automated child support enforcement programs. Eventually, all states' computer systems will be linked to each other.

The information contained in this book applies generally throughout the United States. Because we are most familiar with California's child support system, and because California maintains the largest child support caseload in the United States, California's laws and procedures are highlighted in this book. However, all states operate their CSE programs under federal CSE guidelines and regulations. Most of the procedures we describe in this book are used by CSE agencies throughout the United States. Consult your local CSE agency to confirm or clarify any subjects we discuss in this book.

If you, a friend, or a relative have questions relating to child support, or if you have a case that is being handled by a Child Support Enforcement agency, this book will be a valuable tool for you. An attorney might be needed to handle complex legal issues and issues of child custody, child visitation, and property settlements, since CSE agencies do not usually become involved in these subjects.

We have worked in this system. Bonnie White is now a Child Support Enforcement officer who has worked the District Attorney's Office—Family Support Division in Contra Costa County, California, for six years. Douglas Pipes was the former supervising deputy in charge of the same CSE agency for more than five years.

Bonnie White deals directly with both custodial and noncustodial parents on a daily basis. In this capacity, she has become increasingly concerned over parents' lack of knowledge on child support enforcement issues. She came to realize that many parents make serious mistakes that adversely affect their child support cases, often causing major problems that could have been avoided had the parents known what to do.

As the Deputy District Attorney in charge of the Family Support Division of the Office of the District Attorney of Contra Costa County,

California, Douglas Pipes administered a complex bureaucratic agency, responded to parents' complaints and problem cases, worked to keep the CSE agency in compliance with highly regulated government mandates, and wrote and advocated for new laws to simplify and improve an antiquated child support collection system. The authors have joined forces to produce this book in the hope of helping parents make the best possible use of the CSE system.

However complicated or simple your case may be, this book will lead you step by step through the CSE process, enabling you to understand how your case should be handled and what rights you have. This journey through the entire CSE system is a journey you cannot afford to miss.

Chapter 1

The Child Support Enforcement Agency and Its Services

The Child Support Enforcement (CSE) system was created by the federal government in 1975 to facilitate the collection of child support for children who needed support from *both* of their parents. The object of enforcing support obligations was to prevent poverty among children and to reduce welfare rolls.

At its inception, the primary target of federal legislation was the reduction of welfare costs caused by Aid to Families with Dependent Children (AFDC). State departments of social services—the government agencies that supervise welfare programs—referred cases to state-established agencies responsible for child support enforcement. The CSE agency then pursued the absent parents to obtain reimbursement for welfare. It soon became obvious that by collecting child support from noncustodial parents, children could be removed from AFDC.

In the early 1980s, the CSE program was expanded to provide services to custodial parents who were *not* receiving welfare, in order to prevent families from needing to apply for AFDC.

States are required to establish CSE agencies to collect child support for custodial parents who receive welfare and those who do not. The federal legislation was enacted as Section (D) of Title IV of the Social Security Act. Hence, CSE agencies are now called IV-D agencies. The federal government now supervises and regulates the CSE program. States implement the program by enacting their own laws creating and empowering agencies.

New laws have given the agencies more power to enforce child support orders; the advent of computers has accelerated child support collections and caseloads; annual child support collections have increased; and the pace of new welfare cases has slowed.

Money matters

The Nineteenth Annual Report to Congress for the fiscal year 1994, compiled by the National Reference Center—Administration for Children and Families, reported that between 1990 and 1994 the CSE program grew from 12.8 million cases (8 million of which were AFDC cases) to 18.6 million cases (10.4 million of which were AFDC cases). During this period, the non-AFDC portion of the caseload increased by 69 percent, while the AFDC portion grew by 36 percent. Child support collections increased from $6 billion to $9.9 billion. Non-AFDC collections accounted for 74 percent of the total amount collected. It is easy to see how the CSE program has helped reduce the ranks of welfare recipients and saved billions of dollars each year.

The purpose of the CSE

The CSE agency does not represent the custodial parent (the caretaker who has physical custody of the children), the noncustodial parent (the parent who is absent from the home), or the children, although it provides services to each of these groups. The agency is responsible for protecting the financial interest of the taxpayers. Consequently, the state has a vested interest in assuring that child support is paid for these children by the parents, and not by the taxpayers.

All CSE agencies operate under a common set of federal standards through each state's Central Registry, and are required to work together. In California, the local office of Child Support Enforcement is a part of the District Attorney's Office called the Family Support Division or Family Support Bureau. In other states, CSE agencies operate through their Department of Human Services (welfare), the Department of Justice, the state tax agency, or the Attorney General's Office.

To locate your local CSE office, refer to Chapter 9, which lists the name, address, and telephone number for each state's Central Registry, as well as foreign agencies.

CSE services

CSE agencies offer five basic services. They are:

1. Locating the absent parent.
2. Establishing paternity of the father.
3. Establishing child support orders.
4. Establishing medical support orders.
5. Enforcing and collecting child support, spousal support, and medical support orders.

CSE agencies do *not* become involved with custody or visitation disputes, even though the child support order can contain custody and visitation clauses. The Welfare Reform Act contains a $10 million authorization for states to enact programs to facilitate noncustodial parents' access to their children. However, this program might take states years to implement and develop. Until these visitation centers are established, parents must continue to initiate a separate legal action on their own initiative for enforcement of custody and visitation orders.

CSE agencies do *not* create or enforce property settlements, unless the court order specifically provides that property or revenues from the sale of property be used to offset a child support obligation.

CSE agencies do *not* become involved with divorce proceedings, except on child support questions as part of a marriage dissolution. In a marriage dissolution in which the children receive public assistance, the agency must participate in the child support portion of the divorce. In nonaid cases, the custodial parent can request that the CSE office intercede on his or her behalf regarding the child support portion of the divorce. Contact your local CSE agency for clarification on that office's policy regarding involvement in marriage dissolutions.

CSE agencies do not try to prevent parents from harassing each other, nor do they handle restraining orders. The parent who is being harassed must initiate legal action without the involvement of the CSE agency. Harassments and threats should also be reported to the police and courts.

CSE agencies receive child support cases in three ways:

1. The Welfare Department refers all new AFDC, medical-only, or foster care cases to the agency.
2. A custodial or noncustodial parent presents a completed application for nonaid services to the agency.
3. An agency in another state or country refers a child support case to the agency on behalf of the custodial parent or welfare case in the other jurisdiction.

Although each agency has a unique structure, each agency usually consists of two parts:

1. A unit to *establish* child support orders (for example, locating a missing parent, adjudicating the father's paternity of the child, and the establishing of an order for support—see Chapter 5)
2. A unit to *enforce* child support and medical support orders (for example, serving a wage assignment and health insurance order on an employer, recording a child support judgment and filing a property lien, and intercepting state and federal tax refunds, and unemployment and disability benefits—see Chapter 6).

Chapter 2

AFDC Cases (Aid to Families with Dependent Children)

A custodial parent who applies for Aid to Families with Dependent Children (AFDC) is required to submit forms to the CSE agency, asking him or her to describe his or her relationship with the noncustodial parent; provide employment and asset information; criminal history; and names of friends and relatives of the noncustodial parent; and list all child support payments made by the noncustodial parent for the children who are to be granted AFDC.

By applying for aid, the parent assigns his or her right to the CSE agency to collect child support from the noncustodial parent. As long as the custodial parent receives welfare, he or she gives up the right to receive ongoing child support and all past due arrears owed by the noncustodial parent.

When the custodial parent stops receiving AFDC, the government maintains the right to collect unpaid child support arrears from the noncustodial parent up to the total amount of welfare paid. Any past-due child support that *exceeds* the welfare paid for the children reverts to the custodial parent. For example:

> *A custodial mother has an order for child support and is owed $10,000 in past-due support. She loses her right to collect the $10,000 in past-due support until she stops receiving AFDC. If the mother stops receiving AFDC after one year, and the total amount of AFDC paid to her was $7,000, the government maintains the right to collect the $7,000 in back support previously owed to the custodial parent. The agency then pursues the noncustodial parent for the entire amount due, $10,000. Of*

this amount, $7,000 is assigned to the state and the remaining balance of $3,000 is now owed to the custodial parent, in addition to any future payments.

If the total AFDC payments exceed the amount of child support due, the principle of "assignment" allows the government to keep the right to collect *all* past due support previously owed the custodial parent in order to repay welfare costs. The custodial parent in this situation loses the right to collect any of the child support arrears.

Each time the custodial parent receives then stops receiving AFDC, a new "assigned arrearage" must be calculated based on the total welfare payments paid to the custodial parent and children. The most important cause for this on-welfare/off-welfare cycle is the failure by the noncustodial parent to pay child support regularly. Full and regular payment by the noncustodial parent commonly enables most custodial parents to remain off welfare.

When a noncustodial parent begins to pay child support on a regular basis, the amount of child support that is paid can exceed the monthly AFDC payment that is being made to the custodial parent. When the collected child support exceeds the amount of the welfare payment, the *excess* is *passed on* to the custodial parent who will eventually be removed from welfare.

In many states, the CSE agency pursues child support reimbursement back to the date the children were first granted AFDC. If it takes many months to locate the noncustodial parent and establish a child support order, there will be a period of time for which the agency seeks reimbursement for welfare paid on behalf of the children. The agency ordinarily sets child support and reimbursement amounts that are *not* negotiable in AFDC or foster care cases, because these amounts are calculated based on state guidelines. Long delays in establishing a child support order can result in very large reimbursement amounts.

Noncustodial parents who find out their children are receiving government assistance should contact the agency to speed the process of establishing a child support order. Early establishment of an order for support helps avoid the creation of a large reimbursement order and the financial hardship such an order can cause parents. It does not reduce the overall amount of child support owed, but the payments are spread over a longer period of time.

Several years ago, a noncustodial parent came into our CSE office with his tax return and current pay stubs and requested that our agency establish the paternity of his child and begin to collect child support from him. Our staff was surprised at this unusual request. We located the welfare referral form that the custodial parent had completed, and determined that she had been granted AFDC only one month earlier. We calculated the amount he should pay in current child support and what he owed for the one month of welfare reimbursement. He signed a stipulated support order and paid his one-month reimbursement on the spot.

When we asked this man why he voluntarily came to our office, he said that he did not want to be saddled with a huge reimbursement order that would follow him for many years. He said he had tried to pay child support directly to the custodial parent and had encouraged her to get a job, but she told him she didn't want to go to work and would fare better on welfare. This noncustodial parent was not comfortable with his child on welfare, but he couldn't stop the custodial parent from applying for and receiving AFDC. The father believed it was in his best interest to speed up the process of establishing paternity and paying support.

The voluntary assumption of responsibility of parenthood is an event that does not occur as frequently as most child support enforcement specialists would like. Most noncustodial parents whose children become CSE agency cases have either procrastinated in assuming their responsibilities or have deliberately tried to avoid paying child support. Whatever the motivation, the result is the same: children and a custodial parent dependent on welfare, and a noncustodial parent who faces the financial hardship of a large child support debt and unpleasant collection efforts of the CSE agency.

Good cause

Custodial parents who receive welfare are required by law to cooperate with the agency in its efforts to collect child support from the noncustodial parent. Parents who do not cooperate risk the loss of their AFDC payments. However, when the custodial mother's cooperation with the CSE agency threatens her physical safety or the safety of her children, she has the right to sign papers claiming good cause to not cooperate in the collection of support. A verified claim of good cause means that the custodial parent may decline to provide the CSE agency with information on the noncustodial parent and his income and assets, because that parent is likely to seek revenge against her or the children.

Few custodial parents qualify to claim good cause. Verification of such a claim requires a documented history of physical abuse by the noncustodial parent, the existence of a restraining order against the noncustodial parent, and other evidence of violent conduct in the relationship between the parents. A claim of good cause is decided by the Department of Social Services/Welfare Department.

The CSE agency has the right to pursue the noncustodial parent for child support without the assistance and cooperation of the custodial parent, but sometimes it chooses not to pursue the noncustodial parent for fear that he or she will retaliate against the custodial parent and children.

Welfare Reform Act

The Personal Responsibility and Work Opportunity Reconciliation Act of 1996, commonly known as the Welfare Reform Act, has imposed severe restrictions on parents' ability to collect welfare, and has also affected the collection of child support by CSE agencies. For purposes of simplicity, we will call this statute by its popular name, the Welfare Reform Act. (The Welfare Reform Act has renamed AFDC. What was formerly called AFDC will now be called "TANF"—Temporary Assistance to Needy Families. Because the term "TANF" has not yet become a familiar phrase, we will continue to refer to welfare as AFDC in this book. Within the next couple of years, the acronym "AFDC" will be replaced with "TANF.")

The principal purpose of AFDC is to provide temporary financial assistance to families suddenly faced with greatly reduced income or assets. It is intended to be a helping hand until the family is able to regain its financial health. Unfortunately, AFDC has become a "life style choice" for many. Many adult recipients have lost their incentive to become employed and self-supporting. They frequently live in low-income housing projects subsidized through government housing assistance programs, and receive cash assistance, food stamps, and subsidized or free medical services. Over the last 30 years, millions of welfare recipients have grown from childhood to adulthood while receiving AFDC benefits. Some families can trace welfare receipt for three generations.

Some people are so dependent upon AFDC and other forms of welfare that they are unable or unwilling to make efforts to escape the vicious cycle of welfare and poverty. A life of poverty contributes to pervasive illegal drug use, teenage pregnancies, and high dropout rates from school and has caused millions of men, women, and children to become dependent upon government assistance for their basic needs and for survival.

Most welfare recipients live in single-parent households. Many have inadequate educational or technical skills with which to obtain regular employment. Those who obtain employment in an effort to escape welfare often find that they qualify only for minimum-wage jobs, which do not provide them with an income large enough to pay the cost of childcare needed for them to work, and they are forced to return to AFDC.

The intent of the Welfare Reform Act is to stop the cycle of dependency by inducing millions of custodial parents into the work force, some for the first time in their lives. It provides a lifetime cap of five years of welfare eligibility, beginning with the initial date AFDC was granted or effective with each state's enactment of the Welfare Reform Act. Once a parent has used his or her five-year period of eligibility, that parent becomes permanently ineligible for further welfare. States will be able to grant hardship exemptions in individual cases, but only a fraction of people receiving AFDC will qualify.

AFDC and employment

Welfare recipients will be required to obtain employment within two years of their initial AFDC grants. Welfare recipients not employed during the first two years can be required to perform community service for 20 to 30 hours per week. Failure to comply with work requirements will result in either a reduced welfare grant or a termination of benefits. (Some benefits, such as Medicaid and Transitional Child Care, might continue to be offered to recipients who lose cash welfare assistance.) Only parents with children under the age of 6 who lack childcare, or parents who qualify for other state-established hardship programs will be temporarily exempt from penalties for failure to become employed.

Many government agencies and private employers are being urged by the federal government to make efforts to provide employment opportunities for welfare recipients.

The importance of payments from the noncustodial parent

There is no question that a key component—perhaps the single most important component—in helping custodial parents make the transition from welfare dependency to self-reliance will be the receipt of regular and full child support payments from noncustodial parents.

Far too many custodial parents who receive AFDC give less than their full cooperation to CSE agencies. Welfare mothers who are intentionally uncooperative frequently deny knowing where the noncustodial parent lives or works, or the names of his friends or relatives. They may also declare that they do not know the identities of the fathers of their children. Occasionally a mother has become pregnant by a man she hardly knows, and she honestly does not know his name or other identifying information, but this claim of ignorance is frequently false.

Custodial parents receiving welfare are advised to contact the local CSE agency to give all the information they know about the noncustodial parent. Custodial parents receiving AFDC who purposely withhold information about noncustodial parents in order to "protect them" from having to pay support will soon discover "protection" can become their condemnation to poverty and further economic hardship. Effective July 1, 1997, many welfare recipients now have less than four years before their welfare benefits terminate.

Some noncustodial parents in welfare cases are themselves the products of the cycle of poverty. Many are either in prison or county jails; some are homeless and receiving general assistance; and some are receiving drug or alcohol rehabilitation. Many of them have simply vanished from the lives of their children.

It is sometimes impossible to establish a child support order or to collect child support when dealing with a noncustodial parent who has no ability to pay child support. The only choice for a custodial parent in this situation is to become self-reliant. The custodial parent must avail himself or herself of opportunities provided for training and employment assistance.

Many AFDC custodial parents are first-time recipients who were forced into welfare by circumstances beyond their control. Many apply for and receive welfare with every intention of getting off of aid as soon as possible. These custodial parents often succeed in removing their families from the welfare rolls within two years. They utilize many of the services offered by welfare agencies, and return to school to get the training and education they need to enter the work force. These custodial parents are usually more successful in acquiring child support, since they also work very closely with CSE agencies in order to secure and enforce support orders.

The disregard

The Welfare Reform Act has eliminated a long-term staple of welfare—*the disregard*. The disregard was an incentive payment made to a welfare recipient to induce that recipient to cooperate in the collection of child support. The $50 payment was paid to the custodial parent for each month that child support was collected from the non-custodial parent. The idea behind disregard was that paying welfare recipients an additional amount of money, to be taken out of the child support collected and that would not reduce the welfare grant, would act as an incentive for recipients to cooperate with the agency in collecting support.

Many child support enforcement professionals felt that the disregard simply constituted an additional welfare payment. As soon as each state fully implements the welfare reform changes, it will no longer be required to pay disregard. The incentive for a welfare recipient to cooperate with the CSE agency will be the receipt of child support payments from the noncustodial parent.

Arrearages

Prior to the Welfare Reform Act, any collections that were available to pay arrearages were used to pay welfare arrears first, and nonaid arrears were paid only after welfare had been fully reimbursed.

Beginning Oct. 1, 1997, any child support payments collected in a case in which the custodial parent is no longer on welfare will be sent to the family to pay arrearages that built up after the family stopped receiving AFDC. Only after nonaid arrearages that occurred *after* the family stopped receiving AFDC have been fully paid will child support payments be applied to reimburse the government.

Beginning Oct. 1, 2000, this formula will be applied to the use of support payments to pay arrearages that built up *before* the family received AFDC. However, support payments received while the family *currently* receives welfare will be retained by the government.

Also beginning Oct. 1, 2000, collections for support arrearages will be applied first to arrearages accruing *after* the family stopped receiving AFDC, then to the period *before* the family received assistance, and finally to the period *while* the family was receiving AFDC.

The Welfare Reform Act will produce a massive restructuring of the present welfare and child support enforcement system. Its full implementation will take time, and many of its changes are likely to be introduced gradually. Further changes affecting CSE brought about by the Welfare Reform Act will be discussed as appropriate in other chapters of this book.

Foster care

Many thousands of children live in foster care facilities. Some live with a relative and qualify for foster care status; others live with foster parents, in group homes, or in rehabilitation centers. Caretakers of foster children are called Custodial Persons. Foster care cases are automatically referred to the CSE agency for collection of child support from both parents, because both are considered noncustodial parents. Foster care rates range from a few hundred dollars per month per child to more than $4,000 per month, in unusual cases. The agency usually makes a separate evaluation of each parent's financial ability to pay support, even when they reside together. This process results in a support order for each parent, based on his or her ability to pay support, and produces a separate case in the agency for each parent. As with AFDC, there can be reimbursement costs owed in foster care cases. Delays in the establishment of foster care support orders are common.

When a child support order exists at the time the child enters into foster care, the parent with the order continues to pay according to his or her support order. The payee simply changes from the custodial parent or AFDC account to the foster care account.

The agency must then establish a child support order for the former custodial parent. If he or she is an AFDC recipient, that parent is considered unable to pay support. If he or she is not an AFDC recipient, child support is calculated based on the same criteria normally used to establish a support order.

Foster care cases do not result in an assignment of the former custodial parent's right to collect child support from the other parent. Moreover, the government is not allowed to retain child support collected from parents when that amount exceeds the total amount paid. Should both parents' combined orders exceed the amount being paid monthly for foster care, the amounts are adjusted to equal no more than the total cost of foster care.

The manner in which child support orders are calculated and determined is discussed in Chapter 5.

Medicaid and other federally funded health programs

Custodial parents who are employed in low-income jobs and lack health insurance coverage are eligible to apply for federally funded Medicaid benefits. As with AFDC cases, medical-only cases are referred by the welfare department to the CSE agency to adjudicate paternity when necessary. Custodial parents in medical-only cases have the right to choose whether they want the agency to also establish and enforce the child support obligation from the noncustodial parent. In many instances the noncustodial parent already pays child support directly to the custodial parent and the custodial parent may choose to decline these services.

Because the costs of providing federally funded health insurance to children are paid by taxpayers, the agency establishes orders that require noncustodial parents to obtain insurance for their children. Requiring these benefits to be provided by the noncustodial parent enables the children to be removed from the government-funded Medicaid program.

Some intact families, in which both parents live with each other and with the children, apply for Medicaid. One or both parents are employed, but do not qualify for health insurance through their employment. In intact family cases, the agency adjudicates paternity where necessary, establishes a health insurance order for the employed parent, and then closes the medical support case, since the parents do not have the ability to obtain health insurance.

In medical support cases involving an employed parent who is absent from the home in which the children live and whose employment does not provide health insurance for its employees, the noncustodial parent can be required to apply for private health insurance benefits for the children, as long as the cost of private health insurance is considered "reasonable."

The process followed by agencies in establishing and enforcing health insurance orders is discussed further in Chapter 3.

Minor-mothers (children who bear children)

Each year thousands of teenage girls, some as young as 12 years old, enter into the AFDC system because they become pregnant. These girls are eligible to receive welfare benefits for their children because the fathers are almost always noncustodial. Many of the fathers are also teenagers still attending high school, and are frequently unable to pay child support because of their lack of income.

The cases of teenage mothers are commonly called "minor-mother" cases. They are automatically referred to the CSE agency by the welfare department.

When the agency receives a minor-mother referral, it begins legal proceedings against three parties: the father of the minor-mother, the mother of the minor-mother, and the father of the minor-mother's child.

Many parents of minor-mothers are upset when they learn that their daughters are able to receive welfare benefits on their own by becoming pregnant, moving out of the parents' home, and living on their own. Many want their daughters to remain in the family home, to be supported by them, and to remain off welfare.

The conflict in these cases is normally caused by young girls who do not want to live under the control of their parents—they want to manage their own lives. The fact that minor-mothers are not capable of independent living is established by their applications for AFDC. Minor-mothers' need for taxpayer support proves that they are not able to support themselves independently from their parents. Because the parents of minor-mothers are legally responsible to support their daughters until emancipation, they have been targeted by CSE agencies to pay child support for their minor-mother daughters.

Teenage boys who become fathers are frequently shocked to discover that they are obligated to provide child support for their child for at least 18 years.

An increasingly serious social problem is adult men (age 18 or older) who father children of minor-mothers. The paternity of the child can subject an adult father to a charge of statutory rape. Many states now actively prosecute adult fathers of the children of minor mothers. They face years of child support payments, large sums of welfare reimbursement, criminal prosecution for statutory rape, and in some jurisdictions, the requirement to register as sex offenders.

The Welfare Reform Act has enacted important changes for teenage parents and minor-mothers. In order for a minor-mother to be eligible to receive AFDC benefits, she must enroll in high school or a state-approved GED program, and live under adult supervision. The Welfare Reform Act has eliminated the enticement of physical and financial independence from one's parents. Now all minor-mothers receiving AFDC will be required to complete their education and live with a parent or approved guardian.

Another significant change implemented by the Welfare Reform Act is that parents of a noncustodial teenage father (the grandparents of the minor-mother's child) will be liable to pay child support until their teenage son emancipates, if the minor-mother receives welfare. Prior to enactment of the Welfare Reform Act, grandparents were *never* liable to pay child support for their grandchildren, and the government could not collect child support from a minor-father until he became employed.

Unknown fathers

CSE agencies routinely confront the problem of custodial mothers who receive welfare and claim they do not know the identities of the fathers of their children. The vast majority of these cases involve welfare fraud or custodial mothers who do not want to reveal the identities of the fathers.

The claim that the father of her child is unknown almost always causes a CSE agency to conduct an in-depth paternity interview of the mother. Some CSE agencies conduct multiple interviews, and the mother can be required to complete paternity paperwork several different times. The intent of multiple interviews and repeated paperwork is to penetrate false stories.

Such stories range from plausible to outrageous. One common story is that the custodial mother became pregnant by a casual acquaintance while intoxicated. Sometimes they claim that their babies are the product of a rape or sexual molestation. One mother claimed that her pregnancy resulted from sperm injected into the water by an unknown donor in a swimming pool.

Although these women sometimes tell convincing stories, most are broken down by careful investigation, and the noncustodial fathers are identified.

The unknown father often lives in the home with the custodial mother. When he is located living with a custodial mother receiving AFDC on the claim that he is absent from the household, the case is referred to either the prosecutor's criminal division or the welfare department's fraud unit for possible prosecution of both parents.

One common situation in which a custodial mother can honestly state the identity of her child's father as unknown occurs when the mother has had multiple sexual partners during the period of time when the child was conceived. The mother frequently is able to give the agency a list of sexual partners who *could be* the father. The task of the agency is to investigate each possibility and eliminate those men who cannot be the father. This process of paternity adjudication is described in Chapter 5.

Welfare fraud

Some welfare experts have claimed that as many as one-half of all welfare cases involve some type of fraud. The most common form is fraud by unreported earnings. A welfare recipient is required to report all earnings to the welfare department, which considers earnings in determining eligibility for assistance and the level of assistance to be granted. Contrary to popular belief, the average level of welfare grants is not high. Many recipients discover that living solely on AFDC is a difficult task. They sometimes seek to supplement their AFDC grants by obtaining employment in which they are paid cash, and their added income is not reported to the government. Many are caught when their friends or neighbors inform the government of their employment, and investigators confirm the employment and unreported income.

Live-in noncustodial parents

CSE agencies are also required to report to the welfare department any fraud it uncovers. The most common referrals involve live-in noncustodial parents. Such cases occur when the custodial parent claims to have no knowledge of the noncustodial parent's whereabouts, but the noncustodial parent is actually living with the custodial parent. The noncustodial parent is usually employed, while the custodial parent receives welfare, subsidized housing, food stamps, and health insurance, all at taxpayer expense.

One common claim made in welfare fraud is that the noncustodial parent lives with his parents, and this statement is supported by the assertion that the noncustodial parent keeps his or her clothing and receives his or her mail at his or her parent's home. Although this type of fraud is difficult to prove, welfare fraud investigators sometimes surveil the home to establish that the noncustodial parent actually does live with the custodial parent and the children.

When investigators establish that the noncustodial parent spends the majority of his or her time in the home of the custodial parent, or they find evidence that the noncustodial parent's real home is that of the custodial parent, the custodial parent often is criminally prosecuted. If not criminally prosecuted, the custodial parent can be required to reimburse the government for welfare payments he or she received.

False absence

A welfare recipient commits "false absence" fraud when he or she applies for and receives AFDC benefits for children who actually live with the noncustodial parent. Agencies uncover such fraud when they contact the noncustodial parent in establishing a child support order, only to discover that the children live with and are supported by him or her. The agency usually requests the "noncustodial parent" to provide proof of the children's residence, including school attendance records, day-care provider statements, and statements of landlords or friends.

Phony children

Phony children fraud is committed when an applicant receives AFDC for nonexistent children, or when the applicant receives multiple AFDC welfare grants for the same children, using assumed names and different Social Security numbers. Such applicants caught committing this kind of welfare fraud are almost always criminally prosecuted.

Taxpayers are justifiably intolerant of welfare fraud. A citizen can report suspected welfare fraud to either the local prosecutor's office or welfare department. The enactment of the Welfare Reform Act and the increasing automation of welfare and child support enforcement systems are expected to accelerate government efforts to detect welfare fraud. The goal of CSE agencies is to ensure that children receive the full financial support of both of their parents, thus ensuring that no custodial parent believes he or she must commit welfare fraud.

Chapter 3

Nonaid
Cases

Many custodial parents who have child support cases with CSE agencies have first tried to enforce their orders through their own efforts or through the services of an attorney, but have experienced unsatisfactory results. A single parent typically does not have the time and resources needed to track down a noncustodial parent and identify that parent's assets. Custodial parents generally work outside their homes and live on fixed budgets.

Many have waited too long to receive help. Parents who have been unable to enforce their child support orders are often owed thousands of dollars in back child support before they open cases with an agency—approximately 10 million custodial parents who are not receiving any type of government assistance have opened support cases with CSE agencies in the United States.

Any parent can request the services of a CSE agency. Parents who already have a child support order resulting from the dissolution of their marriage can open a case for the purpose of modifying and enforcing the order. The basic service of the agency is to establish a child support order and enforce child and spousal support orders using a multitude of enforcement tools, some of which are uniquely available to these agencies. The federal government has established time schedules in which all CSE agencies must open a case, establish parentage and support orders, and use enforcement mechanisms. The time lines are as follows:

Within 5 days:

- Provide CSE application when requested by telephone or in person.
- Serve a wage assignment within five working days of issuance.
- Re-serve an existing wage assignment within five days of employment verification.

Within 20 days:

- Open a new case and make a record of the actions taken in a case within 20 calendar days from date application or referral was received.
- Initiate interstate action upon verifying that the noncustodial parent is in another state or jurisdiction.

Within 30 days:

- Take appropriate action after verifying new locate information on the location of the noncustodial parent .
- Take appropriate action on a child support account that is 30 days past due.
- Respond to a request from another jurisdiction for information.
- Respond to a parent's written request to provide information.
- Respond to a formal complaint received from a parent or other jurisdiction.

Within 60 days:

- A case identified for closure must remain open for at least 60 days after "notice of intent to close case" letter has been sent to a custodial parent who has not requested that the case be closed.

Within 75 days:

- Check the records of local, state, and federal locate resources if the noncustodial parent has disappeared.
- Provide requested services or information on incoming interstate reciprocal case within 75 days of receipt of case.

Within 90 days:

- File paternity complaint or complete service of process within 90 days of locating a noncustodial parent (or make a record of the locate efforts if service was unsuccessful).

- Establish a support order or complete service of process within 90 days of locating a noncustodial parent and/or of establishing paternity.

Within 365 days:

- Within one year from successful service of process or from when the child has reached six months of age, paternity must be established or the claimed noncustodial parent must be excluded as the parent by genetic blood tests.

Although states are required to meet these federal time schedules, mitigating circumstances—missing or incomplete information submitted by the custodial parent, an unlocated custodial or noncustodial parent, and delays caused by court hearings—can often justify going beyond these specific periods of time.

In order to meet these time schedules, many counties and states have implemented automated or computer-generated letters, delinquency notices, and requests for employment records as a way of staying in compliance with the federal requirements. However, because many CSE agencies do not have automated computer systems, these time schedules are sometimes difficult to meet. Parents must keep in contact with their CSE agencies to make sure that their child support cases are being properly worked within the required time schedules.

Many custodial parents are unaware that a CSE agency can obtain a support order for them, and that they can receive support in as little as 90 to 120 days. Most parents are surprised to find that the services are generally free of charge, although some agencies may require an application fee of no more than $25 from nonaid custodial parents. Most agencies waive this fee; some charge the noncustodial parent.

Supplying the CSE agency with necessary information

If a custodial parent provides incomplete information to the CSE agency, the resulting delay often costs the custodial parent in the form of lost and delayed support payments. Lack of information can cause the caseworker to set the case aside until receipt of needed information, and months can pass before he or she works on it again.

To avoid problems caused by incomplete information, the custodial parent must carefully follow all of the instructions given him or her for opening a child support case. He or she should complete all forms by following the instructions, and provide the agency with the specific and detailed information needed to begin the process. By being thorough, keeping records, and following up when results do not occur in a timely fashion, the custodial parent can be an asset to the CSE agency.

The nonaid custodial parent who opens a child support case should supply the following vital information:

1. The full legal name of the noncustodial parent and all other names the noncustodial parent has used.

2. The date of birth of the noncustodial parent.

3. The Social Security number of the noncustodial parent (if known).

4. The driver's license number of the noncustodial parent (if known).

5. The last known address of the noncustodial parent.

6. The names and addresses of all present and former employers of the noncustodial parent.

7. All known information about the actual and potential assets of the noncustodial parent.

8. Legible copies of all existing court orders that affect the child support obligation, including any marriage dissolution orders.

9. An accurate record of all child support payments already made by the noncustodial parent.

10. The names, dates of birth, and Social Security numbers for all of the children for whom the custodial parent is seeking support.

11. A paternity questionnaire and a birth certificate for each child for whom support is sought, if paternity is at issue.

12. The noncustodial parent's birthplace and his or her parents' names. This data is required by the Federal Parent Locator Service (FPLS) in order to run a Social Security number search for the noncustodial parent.

Although not every custodial parent will be able to provide all of this information, parents should attempt to supply as much of this information as possible in order for the CSE agency to quickly locate the noncustodial parent and his or her assets.

Record-keeping

When the custodial parent does not provide the agency with legible copies of prior court orders and accurate records of child support payments made by the noncustodial parent, the agency must then obtain copies of all prior orders and must request a payment history before beginning work on the case. Providing legible copies of the support orders, along with all other required information, will help minimize delays.

Case opening forms usually require the custodial parent to complete under penalty of perjury a record of prior payments received, because the noncustodial parent is entitled to receive credit for support payments made in compliance with the order. A parent's signature confirms that all the information provided is truthful and complete to the best of the parent's knowledge. A custodial parent who knowingly provides false information is exposed to potential criminal repercussions, and his or her credibility will be suspect.

An effective child support enforcement process requires that both parents keep accurate records. When a custodial parent says that a noncustodial parent has never paid support, the agency will proceed against the noncustodial parent for the full amount owed. If the noncustodial parent produces copies of canceled checks to prove payment, after the agency has seized his or her assets, time is wasted, negative feelings between the parents escalate, and the court may cite the perjuring parent for contempt of court.

All child support payments should be made by check or money order with the words "child support" noted on the front. Noncustodial parents should *always* save money order receipts and canceled checks as proof of payment. Child support should *never* be paid in cash.

Informal modifications of support orders

Both noncustodial and custodial parents should be reluctant to agree to informal modifications that are not ordered by the court and are not in writing. If both parents comply with the exact terms of the court order, the chances of a dispute over money at a later date are greatly reduced. Consider the following scenario:

> *A divorce order sets child support at $500 per month. Both parents verbally agree that the noncustodial parent will pay a monthly car payment instead of writing a check for child support. The parties later have a falling-out. The angry custodial parent opens a case with a CSE agency, claiming that the non-custodial parent never paid support. The agency pursues the noncustodial parent for two years of missed payments. The noncustodial parent states that he paid car payments in lieu of child support, as per the verbal agreement with the custodial parent. The agency probably cannot honor this agreement because the court did not authorize support in the form of automobile payments. The agency will generally fix the arrears due under the court order at $12,000—the full amount of child support not paid.*

To be relieved of this double-payment burden, the noncustodial parent usually must hire an attorney and request the court to release the obligation. Even if the noncustodial parent succeeds in convincing the court to credit the automobile payments as child support, this parent will have incurred litigation expenses, including attorney's fees and lost wages. Parents should not agree to alternate payment arrangements that are not specified in the court order without a formal modification of the order. Until a formal modification of the order is made by the court, the noncustodial parent should pay according to the terms of the order, and the custodial parent can use the payments as he or she chooses.

Function of child support payments

Child support payments are intended to provide a home, food, and clothing for the children, but the courts and CSE agencies do not dictate the manner in which the custodial parent spends the money. Many noncustodial parents feel that their child support payments are not being used to benefit the children. Some believe the custodial parent lives beyond his or her means, while the children's needs go unmet.

Far too many noncustodial parents do not comprehend that many custodial parents still struggle financially, even with child support payments. The cost of raising children is not small. Most custodial parents who have cases with CSE agencies need child support payments from the noncustodial parent just to make ends meet.

A custodial parent who has come to rely upon child support payments in order to meet monthly expenses is faced with a serious financial crisis if the noncustodial parent stops making regular payments. Some custodial parents are forced to file for bankruptcy, some are evicted from their homes, and some find their utilities turned off or cars repossessed. They are often forced to apply for welfare.

Custodial parents are well-advised to budget their expenses without considering child support, because four out of five noncustodial parents fail to make regular payments. Most custodial parents believe that their own earnings are insufficient, however, and once they become accustomed to receiving support, they come to depend on it and can't make ends meet without it.

Noncustodial parents open child support cases, too

Occasionally, a noncustodial parent wishes to open a child support collection case because some custodial mothers refuse to acknowledge the father's parentage, refuse visitation, and sometimes decline the noncustodial parent's offer to pay support. Basically, these women want no contact with the noncustodial parents. The noncustodial father, however, can feel obligated to support his child and might want to develop a relationship with him or her, albeit against the mother's wishes.

Paternity cases initiated by noncustodial fathers are uncommon. Fathers who want to initiate paternity cases should contact the CSE agency to determine whether or not the agency will handle the case. Once the agency determines it can proceed on a paternity case without the cooperation of the custodial parent, and if it finds evidence supporting the noncustodial parent's claim, the agency can begin legal action requiring the custodial parent and child to submit to a blood test. If the man is adjudicated to be the biological father, the court can fix a child support order, and the agency can begin to enforce it.

A benefit to the noncustodial father who opens a child support case with a CSE agency is the creation of a payment record. It also opens the door for the father to pursue a court order, usually in a separate legal action, for visitation and shared custody.

Another reason some noncustodial parents open cases with a CSE agency is that the agency regulates the process of modifying and collecting payments. Some noncustodial parents believe that the custodial parent repeatedly takes them to court over support issues and makes claims that they have not paid child support. Some believe that the custodial parent too frequently requests increases in the level of the order. By opening a case with the agency, noncustodial parents can obtain a measure of protection from such legal actions. The agency monitors payments and initiates modifications in the order only when they are warranted by the income levels of the parents.

Medical support enforcement

Medical support enforcement is another function of CSE agencies. A noncustodial parent can be required to provide medical insurance for the children as part of a support order, if it is available at a reasonable cost through the noncustodial parent's employment. The goal of this system is to protect the children's health and both parents' financial livelihood in a fashion fair to all parties.

The CSE agency typically serves a health insurance order on the noncustodial parent's employer, who is required to implement it. The employer requests the noncustodial parent to complete the paperwork required to begin the coverage. The employer then begins to deduct premiums from the noncustodial parent's pay. The employer is required to send the completed health insurance form to the CSE agency. The form tells the agency what type of insurance has been provided and the policy number. The employer also sends medical cards, claims procedures, and informational brochures provided by the insurance company. The agency forwards the information to the custodial parent who can begin to use the insurance. If the noncustodial parent refuses to cooperate in signing necessary forms and in otherwise assisting in implementing the court-ordered health insurance, he or she can be found in contempt of court.

If health insurance is not offered through the noncustodial parent's employment, the noncustodial parent may be required to seek outside medical insurance coverage if it can be obtained at a reasonable cost. Determining whether the cost is reasonable requires an examination of the noncustodial parent's income and expense statement and a determination of whether the premiums would create a hardship for him or her.

A common problem with some plans is that, although the custodial parent must pay for medical services provided and submit a claim for reimbursement, the reimbursement check is sent to the noncustodial parent. Problems develop when the noncustodial parent keeps the check instead of forwarding it to the custodial parent. The custodial parent, through the CSE agency, is then forced to initiate legal action. This can result in garnishment of the noncustodial parent's paycheck until the reimbursement is fully paid. The noncustodial parent should abide by the child support order and sign over any reimbursement checks for which the custodial parent has fronted the costs.

Some health insurance plans cover the children of the noncustodial parent only if they live in a specific geographical area. Under such a plan, the custodial parent who resides outside of the area has very little recourse against a parent who has kept the children covered under the health insurance policy provided by the employer.

If the needs of the children are better met through the custodial parent's health insurance plan, the court may require the noncustodial parent to pay the custodial parent's insurance premium and a share of any uncovered medical expenses and deductibles. The custodial parent must keep an accurate record of all out-of-pocket medical costs. Should the noncustodial parent refuse to pay his or her share, the agency can proceed against him or her in court to obtain a judgment on these costs.

Spousal support

The CSE agency enforces divorce orders that contain both child and spousal support provisions. Both amounts are combined and enforced together. Normally, remarriage of the custodial parent receiving spousal support terminates the spousal support obligation. Many spousal support orders terminate on fixed dates. For instance, a divorce court can provide that support is to be paid until Dec. 31, 1999, at which time the spousal support obligation terminates.

A custodial parent must notify the agency of any changes that affect the spousal support order. Failure to notify the agency of changes that affect child support, medical support, or spousal support will result in overpayments.

Early notification of pending changes (and following up to be sure change has been implemented) is much simpler than correcting overpayment. Custodial parents must pay back any overpayment through the agency, which then returns the overpayment to the noncustodial parent. The agency can file a legal action against a custodial parent who refuses to cooperate in the return of an overpayment and can obtain a judgment for repayment. Fortunately, most nonaid custodial parents who receive overpayments voluntarily accept withholding of a portion of their current support in order to repay it.

Summary

If you are a custodial parent with a court order for child support, medical support, and/or spousal support, and you have problems enforcing your order, you may open a case with the CSE agency to secure enforcement.

If you have an existing case and are not receiving support payments, contact the agency to determine the nature of the problem and learn how you can assist by providing additional information that can help the agency locate a missing noncustodial parent and seize that parent's assets. Custodial parents should keep accurate records and monitor the results and the progress of their support case on a quarterly basis. Refer to Chapter 6 for information about enforcement of support orders.

Custodial parents who do not have a court order for support should touch base with the agency every six to eight weeks until an order has been obtained and money is being received.

A noncustodial parent needs to keep good records to protect against the loss or destruction of official payment records or to correct errors in those records. Until the last child is emancipated and the child support obligation is terminated, noncustodial parents should keep copies of all canceled checks, money order receipts, and pay stubs reflecting support that has been paid to the custodial parent directly. Noncustodial parents should also save all pay stubs reflecting payments that have been deducted from their wages. The noncustodial parent who discovers errors must take the initiative to provide proof of errors to the CSE agency.

The agency is required to be an impartial third party in *every* case. It is the responsibility of the agency to enforce the child support obligation and protect the rights of children to receive financial support. A noncustodial parent who cooperates with the agency usually avoids costly legal battles and escapes the severe enforcement actions the agency can implement for nonpayment.

The most satisfied parents whose cases are handled by the CSE agency are usually those who have been truthful, fair, and cooperative with the CSE. When both parents believe that they have been treated fairly, when both comply with court orders, and when both have supplied accurate, timely, and pertinent information relevant to their respective positions in the case, the chances are greatly increased that their case will be handled smoothly.

Chapter 4

Locating a
Missing Parent

Noncustodial parents disappear from the lives of their children for as many reasons as can be given for the breakups of relationships. Some noncustodial parents relocate for new employment; some marry or remarry; some move to be near their relatives; and some go into hiding to avoid paying child support.

In order for a CSE agency to obtain a court order for child support, the noncustodial parent must be physically located. The noncustodial parent must be personally served with legal process—commonly a summons and complaint or petition—as the first step in establishing parentage and an order for their support. The CSE agency must also locate the noncustodial parent's assets or sources of income, because it must prove the noncustodial parent has the ability to provide support.

As discussed earlier, it is not uncommon for some custodial parents who receive AFDC to purposefully withhold information on the non-custodial parent's whereabouts. Some AFDC custodial parents protect the noncustodial parent because they believe that child support would not benefit them, since the children are already supported by AFDC. Other AFDC recipients give in to pressures and threats from noncus-todial parents to withhold information on their identities or location. The frequency with which custodial parents withhold information is likely to decrease as more families are removed from the welfare system under the Welfare Reform Act.

Many other AFDC recipients who want to end their reliance on public assistance have participated in training programs to help them regain their independence, and they realize that receiving child support from the noncustodial parent will help them become self-sufficient.

Some custodial parents receiving welfare do not want to have any contact with the noncustodial parent and do not want the agency to find him or her. Some custodial mothers have been physically abused and want to hide from their batterers; some parents want to deny the noncustodial parent contact with their children simply out of spite over the broken relationship; and some parents often fear that the noncustodial parent might abduct the child. As discussed in Chapter 2, custodial parents should claim good cause if they believe their fears are warranted.

A noncustodial parent faced with a custodial parent who wants to deny contact with the children cannot expect help from the agency in establishing contact with the children, because information received by the agency is confidential. The agency will not release the address, employment, or financial information to either parent in a child support case unless requested to do so in writing by both parents. Parents or siblings can send a letter addressed to the other parent in care of the agency. The agency can, but is not required to, forward the letter.

Child abduction and concealment

CSE agencies generally do not involve themselves in cases of child abduction or concealment. However, the agency may, upon request, release information from the case to an agency conducting an investigation into the welfare of the children or into the public assistance received by the custodial parent. A custodial parent who purposely conceals a child's whereabouts from the noncustodial parent can be found in contempt of court in the face of a court order that allows the noncustodial parent to visit that child.

Some custodial parents withhold visitation as a tool to motivate the noncustodial parent to pay support. If the noncustodial parent is not abusive and wants to maintain a relationship, parents sometimes try to negotiate visitation solutions on their own, but efforts are frequently unsuccessful. Some courts provide mediation services to parents to help resolve visitation and custody questions, but when the parents do not reach agreements on these issues, courts must resolve them.

Child abduction by a parent is uncommon, but it does occur. Our agency recently handled a case of a mother who had lost custody of her child to the father because of her drug and alcohol abuse and her failure to provide for the child.

The mother abducted the child from the father's home in another jurisdiction while he was at work. She applied for AFDC in our jurisdiction as a custodial parent, and a child support case was opened in our CSE agency. Our agency notified the father that he should begin to pay support. The father immediately contacted our office and provided us with copies of his custody order and police reports on the child's abduction. Our agency notified the eligibility worker at the welfare department of this development.

Welfare fraud investigators visited the mother's home and found the 4-year-old female child alone in the home with a man. The home contained paraphernalia for drug use. It appeared that the mother wanted to have custody of the child to enable her to qualify for AFDC cash payments, which she could use to support her drug habit. Law enforcement authorities in the jurisdiction where the abduction had occurred were notified of the child's location. The child was returned to the custody of her father and the mother was charged with child abduction and welfare fraud.

The mother was required to repay the welfare she had received for the child and the father was exonerated from any liability for welfare costs incurred during the four-month period in which the mother received AFDC for the child. The father was awarded permanent custody of the child and must continually guard against efforts by the mother to abduct the child.

The Federal Parent Locator Service (FPLS) assists child support enforcement and other state regulated agencies that attempt to locate missing parents and children. FPLS works cooperatively with the Office of Juvenile Justice and Delinquency Prevention to locate parents and children for the purpose of enforcing laws governing child abduction and to enable state agencies to make custody determinations. For more information on this service, contact FPLS through your state's Central Registry as listed in Chapter 9.

Locating a noncustodial parent in a new case

Although physically locating the noncustodial parent can be easier than locating that parent's assets, some noncustodial parents take extreme measures to hide their identities and location. Common hiding tactics include name changes, use of false Social Security numbers, and the establishment of new identities and life styles.

Most CSE agencies have field investigators on staff who track noncustodial parents, serve subpoenas, and execute arrest warrants for noncustodial parents who have been criminally charged for failure to support their children. Many agencies post "wanted" posters showing the photographs and names of parents who have been criminally charged for nonsupport and whose locations are unknown. Some jurisdictions even conduct "fathers' day roundups," in which nonpaying fathers are arrested and brought to court on criminal nonsupport charges.

State Licensing Match System

States have enacted many laws in recent years to enable agencies to locate noncustodial parents, and the Welfare Reform Act mandates states to enact additional laws to achieve this goal.

California has enacted legislation that now requires any person applying for issuance or renewal of a driver's license to provide his or her Social Security number to the Division of Motor Vehicles (DMV). California Vehicle Code section 1653.5 requires that Social Security numbers be obtained in order that a licensed driver who is a noncustodial parent can be located by reference to his or her Social Security number.

This law was enacted to help agencies obtain Social Security numbers of the fathers of children who were conceived during casual relationships. When parents produce a child as a result of a casual relationship, the mother often does not know the full legal name of the father, and rarely knows the father's Social Security number and other data that the agency needs to identify and locate the father.

Another important tool for agencies is their power to induce delinquent noncustodial parents into revealing assets by denying them state-issued professional, business, and driver's licenses. In California, this power is authorized by the State Licensing Match System (called SLMS). Although SLMS is useful in locating a missing noncustodial parent already subject to a support order, its principal effect is to cause the delinquent noncustodial parent to come into compliance with the order.

SLMS works very simply. On a monthly basis, each agency sends a computerized list of the names and Social Security numbers of delinquent noncustodial parents to the State Department of Social Services, or the state agency that supervises the CSE program. The State Department of Social Services compiles the information into a single list, and distributes it to all state licensing agencies. Licensing agencies then check these delinquency lists against all applications for licenses. When an applicant is matched to a name and Social Security number on the list, the licensing agency declines to issue or renew the applicant's license and refers the applicant to the CSE agency that submitted his or her name.

If the applicant does nothing, his or her request for the state-issued license is denied. Many applicants contact the CSE agencies that have submitted their names, and pay off—or reach an agreement on a plan to pay off—arrearages.

If the CSE agency and the noncustodial parent are unable to reach an agreement, the parent has the right to a hearing before a judge or family law commissioner in the jurisdiction in which the CSE agency is enforcing the order.

When the dispute is resolved through voluntary agreement or courtroom resolution, the agency is required to notify the state that the noncustodial parent is in compliance with the order. If the noncustodial parent fails to comply with the new agreement or court order, the agency resubmits the parent's name to the state, and the process of denying license renewal is repeated.

SLMS has proven to be the single most important asset and locate tool for California CSE agencies in recent years. This system has been particularly effective in inducing self-employed noncustodial parents to pay their delinquent child support; but the extension of this program to cover driver's licenses has expanded the scope of its usefulness to include virtually all noncustodial parents. A number of other states have followed California's lead and have enacted similar legislation. For more information on SLMS, please refer to Chapter 6.

Federal case registry

The Welfare Reform Act implemented a federal case registry that, in conjunction with state case registries, provides nationwide child support case tracking. The state and federal registries contain abstracts of all child support orders and information about every case in each state. They will assist in the identification and location of individuals who owe or are owed child support.

Reviewing the application for CSE services

The assigned caseworker reviews the application, which is helpful in developing a profile of the absent parent—a name, approximate age, and physical description. If the application contains very little information, and the child was born out of wedlock, the caseworker usually conducts a paternity interview with the mother of the child, since the first function of a court order for a child born out of wedlock is to establish the legal parentage. This interview often produces additional useful information about the noncustodial parent.

Utilizing the Division of Motor Vehicles

The agency then searches statewide welfare databanks to identify the full legal name and Social Security number of the noncustodial parent. If the caseworker is able to narrow the field of potential fathers to a small list, the CSE can obtain photographs of the men from the DMV, which keeps the photographs that appear on the licenses and identification cards they issue. The caseworker then shows the pictures to the custodial mother. This process of elimination can identify the correct person as the noncustodial parent.

State parent locator services

Parent locator services, which operate in every state and have access to data possessed by numerous other state agencies, can identify a missing parent with as little identifying information as a name, a physical description, approximate age, and the last known city of residence. Even if the service is unable to make a precise identification of the noncustodial parent, it can give the CSE agency a possible "hit"—the name and location of someone who might be the noncustodial parent.

The state parent locator service gets information from the Division of Motor Vehicles, Department of Justice, Employment Development Department, and the State Tax Board. A positive identification of the noncustodial parent by the state parent locator service gives the CSE agency the full legal name, Social Security number(s), driver's license number, date of birth, last known home address, criminal record, and last known employer of the noncustodial parent—usually sufficient data to enable the CSE agency to locate the parent.

State parent locator services previously did not have access to personal data possessed by federal agencies without accessing the Federal Parent Locator Service (FPLS). If the custodial parent did not know if the noncustodial parent was employed by an agency of the federal government, the United States Armed Forces, or the United States Postal Service, it had great difficulty determining employment. Since the agency was unable to locate most noncustodial parents who were federal employees by using state-controlled databases, the CSE had to use FPLS to obtain federal employment information and then had to consult post office and military base records. This process was cumbersome and erratic in its effectiveness.

Federal Parent Locator Service (FPLS)

The agency that filled this gap is the Federal Parent Locator Service (FPLS). It provides to CSE agencies information on federal employees and military personnel by using information supplied by the IRS and Social Security Administration and military records. Although the information provided leads from which the agency could begin its search, the most current information obtained from FPLS reports was already one- or two-years-old when received by the agency. The age of the information rendered the report useless, unless the noncustodial parent had been employed by the same federal agency for a long period of time.

The Welfare Reform Act has mandated an overhaul of FPLS. Now each federal agency will be required to report quarterly to FPLS the names, Social Security numbers, and wages paid to its employees.

The only exceptions will be when disclosure might jeopardize the safety of the employee or compromise an ongoing investigation or mission (such as for an intelligence officer).

The Welfare Reform Act also mandates that FPLS establish a *National Directory of New Hires* to supplement the new hire-directories that each state must establish. The hiring of *federal* employees will be reported to the *Federal New Hire Directory*. Both registries will contain information on child support cases and be updated regularly.

All employers must report the names, addresses, and Social Security numbers of new hires, and the state in which the employees have been hired. Employers will face fines of up to $500 or more for failure to report new hires, for submitting false information, or for conspiring with a newly hired employee to not supply the required report.

The Welfare Reform Act requires the FPLS to send employer and employee information in the *National Directory of New Hires* to the Social Security Administration (SSA). The SSA will be required to verify the accuracy of or supply correct Social Security numbers, dates of birth, and employer identification numbers on all new hires nationwide. This process will assist agencies in locating noncustodial parents for the purpose of paternity establishment and enforcement, or modification of a support order. The information provided by the SSA will be compared with the information provided by state and national directories and FPLS.

Custodial parents do not have to open a case with a CSE agency in order to utilize FPLS. Custodial parents can contact their state's Central Registry (see Chapter 9) and obtain the telephone number for the FPLS in their state if they choose to locate the noncustodial parent on their own.

Locating a noncustodial parent in an existing case

Until state and federal agencies affected by the mandates of the Welfare Reform Act are able to fully implement its programs, it is useful for custodial parents to know of the many ways they can assist the agency in locating a missing noncustodial parent.

If the parents were previously married to each other or lived together, the custodial parent can provide to the agency any personal records left behind by the noncustodial parent—tax returns, hospital records, pay stubs, canceled checks, bank statements, an expired driver's license, letters from family and friends, credit reports, applications for credit, and insurance policies. These records can provide the caseworker with such information as the noncustodial parent's Social Security number, bank account number, last known employer, and the names and addresses of relatives and friends.

Former neighbors of a noncustodial parent also can be very helpful, as some noncustodial parents give information to their neighbors about future plans that they have refused to disclose to authorities. It is also not uncommon for a CSE officer to telephone a friend or relative of the noncustodial parent and discover that the person answering the telephone is the noncustodial parent.

Former employers can also provide valuable information on a noncustodial parent. Because an employer is required by law to mail a W-2 form to every employee, the former employer might have a current mailing address for the noncustodial parent.

Many noncustodial parents have criminal records. CSE agencies are able to check criminal history information (called rap sheets) to find parents who are currently incarcerated, on probation, or on parole. Although an incarcerated parent normally has little or no ability to pay child support, the agency can obtain a paternity adjudication and determine the anticipated release date—a noncustodial parent who has been released from custody might return to the work force and eventually regain the ability to support his or her children.

When the CSE agency locates a noncustodial parent living in another state, the agency can request a copy of that state's parent locator report, which often reveals that the noncustodial parent is living a productive life. Armed with this information, the CSE agency can initiate an interstate action to establish and/or enforce a child support order.

It is not uncommon for a noncustodial parent to move to another state before the agency is able to serve him or her with an interstate action. CSE agency officials hope that future uniform nationwide automation of operations will help reduce the delays caused by such moves.

Although a qualified private investigator can expend large amounts of time to track a missing person who is using an assumed identity, the cost of such an effort makes this option available only to those parents who have plentiful resources and are willing to spend them. A custodial parent who does not want to wait for the CSE agency to locate a missing noncustodial parent can hire a private investigator to run a "quick locate" search for a reasonable fee. The custodial parent can then turn over the information generated by the private investigator to the CSE agency for enforcement.

Although the CSE agency may take longer to locate a noncustodial parent, it still provides the best option for most custodial parents to locate the noncustodial parent and to establish and enforce a child support order against that parent. And the service of the CSE agency is generally provided to the custodial parent without any charge. CSE agencies have access to almost every database possessed by governmental agencies, which helps agencies locate even the most elusive parents.

The intent of the Welfare Reform Act is to circumvent the efforts of noncustodial parents to hide from their obligations. CSE agencies are under federal and state mandates to give high priority to locating errant parents and requiring them to be accountable for the welfare of their children. We suspect that full implementation of the provisions of the Welfare Reform Act will greatly reduce the opportunities for parents to escape their duties to support their children.

Chapter 5

Child Support
Establishment
Procedures

Once the noncustodial parent has been located and the child support agency has an idea of that parent's employment and assets, the agency begins to establish a court order for current support and medical support. If the parents were not married to each other at the time the child was conceived, paternity of the child must be adjudicated. If AFDC is involved, reimbursement for welfare may be sought as well.

Entitlement

A summons and complaint (or petition) is prepared by the CSE agency and filed with the court as the first step in the process of obtaining a court order. A *complaint* or *petition* is a legal document filed with the court that describes the legal action being brought against a defendant and requests that an appropriate resolution of the case be made against the defendant named in the complaint or petition. The title of the case (called the *entitlement*) is assigned to the complaint, and typically reads, "The County of (name of initiating county) on behalf of John Doe Jr., minor child, v. John Doe." If more than one child is involved, the complaint reads, "on behalf of minor children." If the child has not yet been born, the complaint reads "on behalf of an unborn child."

Many states use the custodial and noncustodial parents' names in the case title (for example, "Jane Doe v. John Doe." Child support orders obtained in marriage dissolution actions retain the entitlement of the dissolution action, such as "Jane Doe v. John Doe," using the exact language as was contained in the underlying marriage dissolution petition.

If the complaint was filed for a child who was unborn when the complaint was filed, the birth and naming of the child does not change the entitlement of the case. The title usually continues to contain the language "an unborn child." However, the text of any court orders following the birth of the child will contain the child's legal name and date of birth.

The clerk of the court assigns a docket number to the action, which becomes the identifying case number for the life of the resulting court order. The same entitlement and docket number is used to identify all papers filed in the case with the clerk of the court.

Summons and complaints

The summons is a court order that informs the defendant in a civil action that he or she is being sued, informs the defendant of the nature of the legal action, and advises the defendant of the options available to respond to the suit.

The CSE agency prepares the summons and complaint (or petition) for paternity and child support and sends the documents to be personally served on the noncustodial parent. Many agencies send these documents to the sheriff's department in the county or jurisdiction where the noncustodial parent resides. If the sheriff is unable to serve the papers on the noncustodial parent, the sheriff returns the summons and complaint to the CSE agency, which uses its own personnel or hires a private company that serves process.

If the agency does not have a physical address for the noncustodial parent's residence or if that parent evades service of process, the agency may serve the summons and complaint at that parent's *known* place of employment. If the noncustodial parent is not available to accept service at his or her place of employment, the documents can be served on the parent's employer, requiring the employer to deliver the summons and complaint to the noncustodial parent. This type of service is called "substitute service." A noncustodial parent who knows that he or she is the subject of a child support action can avoid the embarrassment of being served at work by calling the CSE agency or sheriff's department and making arrangements to accept service at an alternate location.

Substitute service can also be effected after several attempts of personal service have been made on a verified address. The process server can deliver the summons and complaint to anyone who answers the door at the defendant's home—whether it's a friend, roommate, or relative.

A claim by the noncustodial parent that he or she was not personally served with a summons and complaint might be difficult to establish, since the CSE agency usually has substantiating proof of the noncustodial parent's employment or residence and can show that the legal requirements for substituted service have been fulfilled.

However, process servers sometimes serve the person who answers the door at the noncustodial parent's residence without verifying that the address and sub-service is proper. In these instances, once the noncustodial parent is notified (usually by garnishment of wages as a result of a default judgment) and can prove that he or she was not properly served, the noncustodial parent must then file a motion to "set-aside" the default judgment based on improper service. If the default judgment is set aside, the process of establishing a child support order must begin again.

Long Arm Service

Another exception to the requirement that a summons and complaint be personally served is when the noncustodial parent resides outside of the state in which the action is filed. The agency usually sends the summons and complaint to the noncustodial parent by certified mail, with a return receipt requested. When the noncustodial parent signs for the papers, the certified receipt becomes the proof of service.

This type of service is called Long Arm Service. It can reach a noncustodial parent anywhere in the United States. If the noncustodial parent refuses to sign the certified letter, and the mail is returned undelivered to the child support agency, the agency can send the documents to the county sheriff in the jurisdiction where the noncustodial parent resides, for personal service.

Summons and complaints for minors

When the noncustodial parent is younger than 18 years of age, the agency must also personally serve a second summons and complaint upon the minor's parent or legal guardian, stating that the defendant is a minor. Serving the parent or guardian assures that the person who is responsible for the minor is aware of the proceedings. Parents of a minor served with an action for paternity and child support can contact the agency to determine the nature of the legal action and decide upon an appropriate answer.

Advice for the custodial parent

A custodial parent is well-advised to keep informed of the status of the agency's efforts to serve the noncustodial parent, by telephoning the agency periodically. If the agency has been unable to serve the noncustodial parent with the summons and complaint, the custodial parent can sometimes arrange for the papers to be served through a friend or relative. The custodial parent can often alert the agency of the noncustodial parent's schedule or present whereabouts. The combined cooperative efforts of the CSE agency and the custodial parent usually result in successful service of process upon the noncustodial parent.

Options upon service of a summons and complaint

A noncustodial parent who has been served with a summons and complaint (or petition) for child support should carefully read the legal papers attached to the complaint to get instructions on what he or she can do. Service of a summons and complaint provides two options. The noncustodial parent must respond to the complaint by: 1) filing an Answer, or 2) signing a Voluntary Stipulation. Failure to respond will result in a default judgment. In California, a person who is sued has 30 calendar days (including Saturdays, Sundays, and holidays) in which to decide what response to make to a complaint for child support.

Stipulation

A noncustodial parent who wants to reach an agreement can call to make an appointment with the agency that filed the complaint. The parent should then bring copies of his or her pay stubs and most recent tax return, so the agency can confirm the accuracy of the wage and income information they may have. If the noncustodial parent agrees to pay the amount calculated by the agency, he or she can stipulate (agree) to a child support order while in the agency office, and avoid having to appear in court to contest the action.

By talking to the agency the noncustodial parent remains free to decline signing an agreement and learns the exact amount of support the agency will request in court.

Filing an Answer

A man who does not agree that he is the biological father of a child, or who has declined to reach an agreement with the agency on an amount for child support, must file with the clerk of the court an Answer or response to the complaint. "Filing" an Answer means that the document has been officially received into the court action.

The clerk commonly requires a defendant in a civil action to pay a filing fee at the time the Answer or response is filed with the court. Filing fees vary from county to county. Parents who are unable to pay the cost of the filing fee can request that the filing fee be waived by the clerk's office. A noncustodial parent can determine the amount of the filing fee or request a waiver by asking either the clerk or the CSE agency.

A noncustodial parent is not required to hire an attorney in order to file an Answer, but a case involving unusual circumstances or legal issues that can complicate the resolution might require an attorney. The CSE agency and county clerk's office usually are able to explain the procedures for filing an answer. However, they are forbidden by law from giving legal advice or assistance to litigants.

It is insufficient to file an Answer by simply completing the Answer form and mailing it to the CSE agency. The Answer must be filed with the clerk of the court that issued the summons. A noncustodial parent who does not reach an agreement with the agency and does not file an Answer generally suffers a default judgment, usually for parentage and child support entered by the court without the participation of the noncustodial parent.

A man named as a father in a child support action who doubts his paternity should always request blood tests and file an Answer denying paternity, unless the agency agrees to allow the defendant to take blood tests without first filing an answer. The judge usually delays the case until the test results have been received. The noncustodial parent is not required to hire an attorney to undergo blood tests, but he or she is always entitled to hire an attorney or consult a paralegal clerk.

Procrastination should be avoided in a child support action since, it can lead to a default judgment. A man falsely named as a father can avoid years of litigation and expense by immediately requesting blood tests to confirm whether he is the father.

Answers vs. stipulations

A noncustodial parent who has already acknowledged paternity of a child but disagrees with the *amount* of child support must file an Answer contesting the amount. This causes the case to be determined by a judge or administrative officer. Again, a noncustodial parent is not required to hire an attorney. Judges use the same state guidelines in determining child support as do CSE agencies, but they are sometimes more flexible than agencies in deviating from state guidelines.

Unless the noncustodial parent is able to show legal and sound reasons why the amount should be lower than the state-enacted amount, he or she should reach a stipulation with the CSE agency to save attorney and court fees.

In most cases in which paternity is acknowledged, the noncustodial parent is employed, and there are no mitigating circumstances justifying a reduction in child support, the best choice is to stipulate.

Noncustodial parents must beware of those persons, including attorneys, who counsel them to fight a proposed child support order without having a sound legal reason for that disagreement. Some attorneys encourage noncustodial parents to litigate simply to increase their own profits. You should request that the attorney explain the legal rationale that would suggest deviation from support guidelines. The noncustodial parent who loses a courtroom fight over the amount of child support ends up paying the amount dictated by state guidelines in addition to attorney fees and court costs.

The noncustodial parent named in a complaint can contact his or her local CSE agency to obtain information and instructions on how to file an Answer or how to sign a stipulation for support.

Administrative process

Many states use the administrative process instead of the judicial process when establishing or enforcing child support orders. Administrative process expedites the child support order by bypassing the delays attendant to court proceedings. The Welfare Reform Act requires all states to implement expedited administrative processes in establishing paternity and child support orders and modifying and enforcing child support orders. Agencies will now be empowered to obtain blood test orders, child support orders, and various enforcement mechanisms without court orders signed by a judge. In many instances, child support commissioners will handle all agency cases. For cases not handled by a CSE agency, parents can use a family law facilitator instead of a judge.

An expedited administrative process will also allow the filing of a simplified Answer by the noncustodial parent. In an expedited administrative process, the summons and complaint sets the amount of child support based on the income information about the noncustodial parent contained in the CSE agency's files. If the noncustodial parent fails to file an Answer or voluntarily stipulate, a default judgment will be entered for the amount requested in the summons and complaint. Contact your local CSE agency immediately if you are served with a summons and complaint or petition that contains a requested judgment for child support. The agency can answer questions regarding the expedited administrative process and explain the available options.

Disputing paternity

Paternity cases, increasing in frequency, are potentially at issue if the parents of a child were not married to each other when the child was conceived. Paternity is only infrequently an issue for a child born when the mother and named father were married to each other at the time of the child's conception, based on the presumed fidelity of married couples. This presumption, however, sometimes conflicts with the reality that married couples do not always remain faithful to one another.

When the parties were married to each other at the time of conception and the custodial mother names her husband as the father, paternity is not normally questioned. A man who believes that a child is the result of his wife's extramarital affair must file an Answer disputing paternity and request blood tests in order to determine whether he is the biological father.

If the parents were not married to each other at the time a child was conceived, a paternity interview is commonly necessary. Paternity interviews ask the custodial parent personal and sensitive questions regarding the conception of the child. A custodial mother who wants to avoid this interview should carefully complete and return all of the paternity forms given to her by the agency.

There have been instances in which a child support order was entered against a father who, at the time of the order, believed he was the true biological father. He later learned that the mother had an affair and he may not be the biological father of the child for whom he has been paying support. When this situation occurs, the legal father must choose whether to attempt to change the court order. This usually requires that the man hire an attorney, request blood tests, and explain to the court why paternity is being disputed.

If blood tests confirm that he is not the biological father, the court should be able to set aside the judgment of paternity and the child support order, particularly if the man had been intentionally misled.

Even if he is relieved of duty to provide child support, a man who was once the legal father of a child might not be able to recover the support he already paid. Some states however, limit the time for a legal father to initiate an action to reverse a paternity judgment. Because states have different time restrictions and rules for resolving paternity issues, noncustodial parents who intend to dispute paternity after the fact should contact an attorney for legal advice.

An occasional court has denied a request to set aside a judgment of paternity and the accompanying child support order on the grounds that the adjudicated father has developed and maintained a long-term relationship with the child, and overturning the judgment is not in the best interests of the child. The whole subject has provoked bitter legal controversy. Its final resolution is not clear.

Repayment of years of child support to a wrongly named father is usually an impossible task for the custodial mother. A judge faced with this situation might simply terminate ongoing child support payments and decline to order repayment of support already paid to the mother. A wrongly named father who has paid child support under a court order might file a civil lawsuit against the mother for repayment of the support payments. The advice of an attorney is usually essential.

The Welfare Reform Act and some state laws no longer allow the custodial parent to name the noncustodial parent on the birth certificate without an acknowledgment of paternity by the noncustodial parent. Before a man becomes liable to pay child support his paternity must be judicially established.

Many parents falsely believe that listing the father's name on their child's birth certificate establishes the paternity of that claimed father. Naming the noncustodial father's name on the birth certificate does *not* legally establish paternity. As a result of the many court challenges brought by defendants who were wrongly named on the birth certificate, the Welfare Reform Act requires all states to enact programs with hospitals in which a noncustodial father can sign a voluntary declaration adjudicating his paternity at the time of the child's birth. (In California, this program is called the Paternity Opportunity Program (POP).) This program should assist states in meeting the federal mandate that all state agencies establish paternity on all children born out of wedlock. If the noncustodial father declines to sign a voluntary acknowledgment, the custodial parent is not to be allowed to list the alleged father's name on the child's birth certificate. This paternity declaration form is also available through many prenatal clinics.

Noncustodial fathers are allowed 60 days to rescind a voluntary paternity declaration if a mistake has been made, and an extra two years if fraud, a material error, or duress is established. A paternity declaration signed by a minor-father will not become a paternity judgment until 60 days after he has emancipated.

Establishing a child's paternity has a benefit to the child that is independent of the ongoing financial support that a judgment of paternity produces. A legal judgment of paternity can entitle a child to receive a portion of the father's estate, titles, or inheritance. The adjudication of paternity can help protect a child from the efforts of members of the father's family to exclude the child from a portion of the father's inheritance on the ground that the child was born out of wedlock and has not been acknowledged by the father.

The child of a deceased father has rights to survivor's benefits and Social Security benefits paid by the federal and state governments. These potential benefits for a child that can result from an adjudication of paternity are considered so important that adjudication of paternity has been made a mandatory function of CSE agencies.

Several years ago, our agency handled a case in which an unwed custodial mother on welfare had four children by the same noncustodial father. When questioned by CSE staff over a five-year period, this parent denied knowing where the noncustodial father lived or worked. The mother provided enough data to our agency to prevent her from being penalized for withholding information, but she did not give us enough to enable the agency to pursue the noncustodial parent to adjudicate the paternity of their four children. Our staff did not believe this mother was being truthful. Even after we explained the need to protect the children's rights by adjudicating paternity, the mother continued to claim that she had no knowledge of the father's whereabouts. She claimed that each of the four conceptions of her children by this man were the result of casual and unplanned sex with him.

About one year after our last conversation with the mother we learned that the noncustodial parent had been killed. The custodial mother went to the Social Security office to apply for death benefits for her four children. Because there was no court order adjudicating paternity and no other documentation substantiating the mother's claim that the children had been fathered by the deceased man, the custodial mother's claim for benefits was denied.

When the custodial mother demanded that our agency contact the Social Security Administration to substantiate her claim, we reminded her about our interviews in which we had advised her to adjudicate the paternity of her children. The mother realized that by inaction and cover-up she had caused her children to face a lifetime of poverty, and had deprived them of their claims to their father's inheritance and Social Security death benefits. All of this was the result of a misguided attempt to protect the noncustodial father from paying child support.

We hope this discussion will give you a better idea of the importance of paternity adjudication in protecting potential financial resources.

Blood tests

If a man named as a father of a child questions whether he is the biological father, he should give serious consideration to paternity blood testing. The average cost ranges from $200 to $400 for a test that compares genetic markers in the mother's, the child's, and the alleged father's blood. If the custodial parent is currently receiving AFDC, the tests can usually be performed without a down payment of fees. Payment will not usually be requested unless the results establish paternity of the named father. If the results of the testing establish that the named father is not the biological father, he is usually relieved of any obligation to pay the costs of the blood testing and that man is excluded as the biological father on AFDC cases. Blood tests are paid for by the noncustodial parent only when the test proves his paternity.

In paternity cases involving multiple sexual partners, in order to establish which person on the list of a mother's sexual partners is the true biological father of a child, the CSE agency usually begins its search with the man deemed to be the most likely possibility. Paternity is established by process of elimination and the CSE agency commonly waives payment of blood test costs until the father has been identified by the testing.

The level of certainty of the identification can usually be stated as such a high percentage that virtually no other man in the world would be biologically capable of being the father. Thus, it is readily accepted that most courtroom challenges to the process are unsuccessful.

Blood testing was challenged in a case recently handled by our agency, which identified a father for whom we had searched for 17 years. When this man was located he laughed about the length of time it took to find and identify him and remarked about how fortunate he was that he would only have to pay child support for six months before the child turned 18.

When he learned that he would have to pay back child support to reimburse the government for AFDC the child had

*received, he decided to contest. He hired an attorney and sub-
mitted to genetic blood tests, which identified him as the father.
He then challenged the method of testing and lost that fight,
too. The father's next argument was that he shouldn't have to
pay welfare reimbursement costs, because the custodial mother
had concealed the child from him; he lost that argument also.
After five years contesting in court, when the child was 22, he
was ordered to pay $20,000 for reimbursement of welfare costs
paid by the taxpayers to support the child.*

By waging a legal war over a biological issue that can be readily
determined, the man probably doubled the financial cost.

Intact families

In an intact family the alleged father, mother, and children reside
together. Intact family cases are usually referred to the CSE agency
by the welfare department. When the family applies for either cash or
medical assistance, and paternity has not been determined, a referral
is made to the CSE agency in order to adjudicate paternity. The
referral is sent in order to establish paternity, because the children
are receiving AFDC as part of a family unit, or because they are
receiving Medicaid.

The agency initiates these cases in much the same way it initiates
all others: The father is served with a complaint naming him as the
father of the children and a summons requiring him to answer the
complaint or resolve the legal issue with the agency.

The father can acknowledge paternity by meeting with agency
staff and signing a stipulation that adjudicates him as the legal
father. Because the parents of the children live together, a current
support order is unnecessary.

If the father in an intact family receiving welfare does not voluntarily sign a stipulated paternity adjudication and does not file an Answer with the court, a default judgment of paternity will be entered
against him. In an intact family case, a default judgment can produce
the same result as a voluntary stipulation—paternity is adjudicated.
Because paternity is not disputed and child support is not at issue, a
paternity adjudication in an intact family is the only situation in
which a default judgment usually does not have a financial impact on

the noncustodial parent. After paternity has been adjudicated, an intact family case is usually closed by the CSE agency.

In any situation in which the named noncustodial parent is unsure of his paternity of the child or child support is an issue, the noncustodial parent makes a serious mistake by allowing a default judgment to be entered against him.

Default judgments

A default judgment is a judgment that is entered without the participation of the defaulting party, which means the defendant has failed to properly answer the complaint either by filing an Answer with the court or by voluntarily stipulating to a child support amount. The usual reason for a default judgment is that the noncustodial parent fails to appreciate the importance of filing an Answer and simply ignores the complaint. Another common cause is that the noncustodial parent mails his or her Answer to the CSE agency without filing it properly with the clerk of the court.

We have difficulty understanding a parent who does not want to participate in the adjudication of paternity and the setting of a child support order. Even the father who acknowledges paternity and the duty to pay support should be interested in ensuring that the court order be for the correct amount. In order for the agency to correctly set child support, the agency must have accurate financial information about the assets, income, and expenses of the noncustodial parent. If the agency is forced to act on information gathered without the participation of the noncustodial parent, the order may be set in an inappropriate amount.

Many noncustodial fathers who have been served with a summons and complaint or petition for child support telephone the agency to deny paternity of the child. There is no such thing as a verbal Answer to a complaint for child support. If a written Answer is not correctly filed with the court, there is no Answer in the case, and a default judgment can be taken against the defendant. Ignoring a civil action for paternity and child support is a very serious mistake. Situations like the following commonly occur:

An AFDC custodial mother names several men as possible fathers. The agency selects the most likely candidate based on the mother's story and proceeds against that man. (The agency some-times elects to determine the possible paternity of the man who is the easiest of the named possible fathers to serve with a summons and complaint.)

The man who is served first with a summons and complaint may fail to file an answer, although he verbally claims he is not the father and even writes a letter to the agency in which he denies paternity. Ultimately, he fails to properly file an answer. Hence, a default judgment is obtained against him.

The judgment adjudicates that he is the father of the child and orders him to pay the government $8,000 in welfare reimbursement, pay current child support of $500 per month, and obtain health insurance for the child. A wage assignment and a health insurance order is served on the man's employer. The employer complies with the orders by deducting the maximum amount allowed (which can be up to 50 percent of the man's take-home pay). The employer will also deduct from his wages the cost of adding the child to the man's health insurance plan.

The man usually phones the agency in anger, claiming that he allowed the default judgment because he didn't know or understand how to prevent it. He often claims that he believed that his telephone call or letter to the agency constituted a proper response. Sometimes he admits that he felt that ignoring the support action would cause it to disappear. He continues to be adamant in his belief that he is not the father of the child.

Because the man was given proper notice of the pending civil suit against him, and because he failed to answer it in the manner required by law, the agency can take the position that the man has agreed that the claims made are accurate, and he has decided to allow the courts to set a support order for him without his participation.

This man now finds himself in a terrible dilemma. He thinks of hiring an attorney, but wonders if he can afford this course of action. On the other hand, he faces the prospect that he will pay child support for a child who is not biologically his. The cost of a child support order is often substantial—a $500-per-month child support order that is effective for 18 years becomes a $108,000 judgment. Unless he is capable of representing himself, the process of maneuvering his case through the legal system is formidable. At the very minimum, this man is usually forced to incur substantial attorney fees to reverse the judgment that resulted from his inattention or inaction.

If this man prevails in the paternity contest, he regains any support money that had been collected under the default judgment, as long as the money was paid to a governmental agency to reimburse welfare costs. But if his support money was paid to a nonaid mother who has spent it, he might be forced to sue the mother to recoup his funds. In the meantime, he has been living on 50 percent of his income for the many months it has taken to overturn the judgment. He probably owes his creditors for bills that were unpaid during this period of reduced income, and his attorney for the fees incurred in representing him.

The CSE agency has expended large sums of the taxpayers' money in obtaining and enforcing a default judgment that is ultimately set aside. The agency still must determine the true biological father of this child, and its process of paternity establishment must begin all over again. This situation could have been avoided had the man responded properly to the civil suit against him.

Even though the maternity of a noncustodial mother is not difficult to establish, a noncustodial mother also errs in allowing a default judgment to be entered against her. She should want to be certain that the amount of support set in the court order is correct. The noncustodial mother who is served with a summons and complaint or petition for child support should give serious consideration to contacting the agency that filed the complaint. In order for the agency to produce a proper child support order, it must know the true income of the noncustodial mother, must know of the mother's other child support obligations or whether she supports other children in her home, and must know what percentage of time to credit the mother for visitation with the child. These facts can reduce the level of the support order.

Because failing to respond to a civil action for child support can cause severe financial consequences, we believe that a noncustodial parent served with such an action should almost never allow a default judgment to be entered against him or her. A parent who wants to dispute the civil action should file a written Answer or response in the court that issued the summons. If the case is only a dispute over the level of support, the noncustodial parent should seriously consider contacting the CSE agency to determine whether it can be resolved without a courtroom proceeding. An out-of-court resolution can often save the noncustodial parent hours of wasted time and can produce a proper stipulated order.

This does not mean, however, that the noncustodial parent should always agree to the amount of support the agency demands. The noncustodial parent who believes the agency has incorrectly calculated the amount or is improperly failing to credit the noncustodial parent for legally recognized hardship reductions can always challenge the level of support in court. A parent may sign a stipulation of paternity and agree with the agency to resolve disputed issues of support in a contested court hearing.

Soldiers and Sailors Civil Relief Act

In 1940 the United States Congress enacted the Soldiers and Sailors Civil Relief Act to enable military personnel on active duty in the armed services to respond to civil actions initiated against them while on active duty.

The process of serving a summons and complaint can often be delayed by difficulties in obtaining a correct address for military personnel on active duty in the armed services. If the noncustodial parent resides in the civilian community, the summons and complaint can be served by certified mail. If the noncustodial parent lives on a military base, the CSE agency can send the summons and complaint to the Office of the Judge Advocate General of that military installation, with a request that the Staff Judge Advocate serve the summons and complaint on the noncustodial parent.

The CSE agency should be able to identify a case in which the noncustodial parent is on active duty in the armed services as a Soldiers and Sailors Relief Act case from the time the case is initiated. A defendant protected by the Soldiers and Sailors Civil Relief Act is allowed the same period of time—usually 30 days—to file an Answer or response to the complaint. If a defendant who is a member of the armed services does not file an Answer for paternity or child support, the agency may *not* obtain a default judgment against him or her. Instead, the agency must request that the court appoint an attorney to represent the absent defendant. The attorney is responsible for contacting the defendant to advise him or her of the action for paternity or support and inform the military member that he or she has been appointed as his or her legal representative.

If the noncustodial parent requests a hearing or paternity blood testing, the attorney can make these arrangements. However, if the noncustodial parent receives but does not respond to letters from the appointed attorney, the attorney may request that the court relieve him or her as counsel for the defendant. Only after the defendant has been given an opportunity to contest the action through appointed counsel, and the defendant has failed to do so, may the agency proceed to obtain a default judgment.

If the agency erroneously obtains a default judgment against an active member of the armed services, it should be set aside, and the procedure required by the act should be initiated.

Additional information about the Soldiers and Sailors Civil Relief Act can be obtained from the Office of Child Support Enforcement (OCSE), a federal agency (see Chapter 9 for contact information). The OCSE can provide a free handbook on child support enforcement affecting persons in the United States armed services. Military personnel already on active duty with the armed services can consult the military legal office (JAG office) on the base where they are stationed. Military attorneys are also usually familiar with the act and can provide free legal assistance to military personnel and their dependents.

Child support guidelines

Because child support guidelines have wide variations from state to state, we will explain them using California as an example. Parents who reside in other states should contact their CSE agency to obtain specific information on child support guidelines in their own state.

In California, the agency may file a civil action to recover back child support for periods in which the child received AFDC. However, California's statute of limitations places a limit of three years on the period for which the CSE agency can recover back child support, calculated backwards from the date the complaint for paternity and support was filed. If the complaint was filed with the clerk of the court on May 1, 1995, but the complaint and the summons was not served on the noncustodial parent until July 1, 1996, the government may seek reimbursement for welfare benefits provided to the child retroactive to

May 1, 1992. However, if the agency does not serve the summons and complaint on the noncustodial parent within three years, it generally forfeits the right to obtain reimbursement for that period.

The CSE agency must have information about the noncustodial parent's income during each year it wishes to set a support or reimbursement order. Agencies are required to periodically send for income reports on noncustodial parents from the state's Employment Development Department and income tax agency. These reports usually cover many years of income, because they often accumulate while the agency attempts to locate and serve the noncustodial parent. If the noncustodial parent has been regularly employed during the period for which the CSE agency can obtain an order of retroactive child support, the amount of reimbursement is likely to be substantial.

The amount of current child support to be paid by the noncustodial parent is determined by a formula established by the legislature in the statutes establishing child support guidelines and generally based on the net pay of the noncustodial parent. When the custodial parent is employed, the formula considers his or her net pay, as well. The amount of the order increases in graduated stages when it covers more than one child. However, the maximum amount that may be collected by garnishment of the noncustodial parent's wages cannot exceed 50 percent of his or her net pay. Any amount exceeding 50 percent accrues as a past-due child support balance.

The child support formula used in California on AFDC cases produces support orders that approximate 25 percent of the noncustodial parent's net pay for the support of one child.

Net pay is determined by deducting state and federal taxes, mandatory retirement contributions (voluntary retirement contributions, such as deferred compensation or 401(k) plans do not qualify), union dues, and health insurance premiums from the gross wages.

The agency then determines the amount of time the noncustodial parent spends visiting the child. A typical visitation credit of 20 percent may be factored in when the noncustodial parent spends 20 percent of the average month with the child. If the noncustodial parent spends more or less than 20 percent of time with the child, the amount may be reduced or increased accordingly.

Once the noncustodial parent's net income has been determined, the agency determines the amount of retroactive child support owed.

If the child has received AFDC, the agency calculates the amount of reimbursement by determining what the amount should have been prior to the filing of the complaint.

Thus, if the noncustodial parent's net pay, after factoring in all of the deductions discussed above, is $2,000 per month, the order for child support should approximate $500 per month for current support for one child.

In the situation discussed earlier in this chapter, the agency would calculate welfare reimbursement for AFDC paid on behalf of the child retroactive to May 1, 1992. If the noncustodial parent averaged $2,000 per month in net income during the period for which reimbursement is sought, and the CSE agency calculated the parent's ability to pay child support at $500 per month, the noncustodial parent would be subject to a $31,000 welfare reimbursement order for the period of May 1, 1992, through July 31, 1997.

However, if the noncustodial parent was unemployed or suffered reduced employment or income during part of the reimbursement period, the retroactive child support order is reduced accordingly. Some agencies calculate a noncustodial parent's ability to pay support on a month-to-month basis. Others average a parent's income over many months or use annual income to determine the long-term ability of the parent to pay support. The latter approach is especially useful when the noncustodial parent's income has significant month-to-month fluctuations.

Because many CSE agencies regularly obtain welfare reimbursement orders, a noncustodial parent who fails to pay child support on an ongoing basis from the time the parent separated from his or her child is only delaying the inevitable. Noncustodial parents can avoid accumulating a large retroactive child support debt by facing up to their support obligations at an early date. Even if the noncustodial parent does not agree with the calculations, he or she should work to resolve the order by agreement with the agency or in court in a timely fashion.

A noncustodial parent who voluntarily pays child support from the first month after separation should keep accurate payment records. If the custodial parent receives AFDC during the separation, accurate records of support voluntarily paid to him or her will likely be credited to any reimbursement order later signed by a judge. Voluntary payment of child support upon separation frequently prevents the custodial parent from needing to apply for public assistance. Thus, the custodial parent avoids the financial hardship and stigma associated with public assistance, the child receives financial support, governmental costs are reduced, and the noncustodial parent avoids a burdensome debt.

Nonaid vs. AFDC cases

One of the most significant differences between a welfare case and a nonwelfare case is that the nonaid custodial parent is not able to obtain a *retroactive* child support order for periods of time prior to the filing of the civil action for child support. Unlike the welfare case where reimbursement for prior welfare payments can be set retroactively, child support in a nonaid case can begin only from the date the complaint has been filed.

The nonaid custodial parent who procrastinates in filing a civil action for support can permanently lose the right to obtain child support from the noncustodial parent for all periods prior to filing the action. The nonaid custodial parent who is separated from the other parent and does not have a temporary or permanent order for child support should quickly begin the process of obtaining an order.

Another difference in a nonaid case is that the custodial parent's income is normally considered in determining the child support order. The greater the custodial parent's income, the smaller the support order is likely to be. The nonaid custodial parent also has the right to negotiate the level of support with the noncustodial parent. Unless the agency determines that the order negotiated by the parents is unjust or endangers the welfare of the child, it usually honors any agreements made by the parents. This means that a nonaid custodial parent may agree to stipulate to a current support order that falls below the level that would otherwise be ordered under the statewide guidelines.

In contrast, a custodial parent who receives AFDC assigns to the government the right to collect child support from the noncustodial parent, and the custodial parent ordinarily has no control over the level of the order. The agency usually follows the state child support guidelines in determining child support orders in aid cases.

Visitation

The credit most child support guidelines give to a noncustodial parent for visitation time provides an incentive for the noncustodial parent to be an active participant in the children's care. The sliding scale that reduces the level of the support order as the percentage of visitation time increases is based on the idea that during the time that a child is visiting the noncustodial parent, he or she is responsible for providing shelter, food, and other necessities.

There is a dispute over the amount of real reduction in a custodial parent's child rearing costs caused by the noncustodial parent's visitation. Many expenses continue regardless of the amount of time the child spends with the noncustodial parent. Moreover, most visitation credit is reserved for regular overnight visits with the noncustodial parent.

On a different note, custodial parents (but usually not custodial persons' relatives) who receive the services of a CSE agency can become parties to child support actions after an order has been obtained. Questions of custody, visitation, and restraining orders can be litigated on CSE agency court orders in some states. Agencies are not required to participate in determining custody or visitation issues, but they are involved in all actions that pertain to child support, unless the nonaid custodial parent makes a written request that the agency close the case.

Nonaid custodial parents who have a CSE agency case may obtain modifications and enforcement of divorce support orders without the written permission of the agency, but if a custodial parent chooses to keep his or her case open with the agency after he or she has taken independent action, the parent must inform the agency of any modifications and turn over or report to the agency any payments directly received from the noncustodial parent.

Childcare costs

The childcare component of child support orders has been a significant development in recent years. Before its implementation, the custodial parent was expected to use a portion of child support to pay for childcare. Costs of childcare have risen so dramatically in recent years that custodial parents had little left to pay for food, clothing, and housing costs associated with the child.

A custodial parent who receives AFDC is not entitled to receive childcare support from the noncustodial parent, because he or she is usually unemployed and has little or no need for childcare.

The nonaid custodial parent who seeks support for childcare must provide proof of monthly childcare costs. The noncustodial parent can be required to pay half of the childcare costs.

Because a nonaid custodial parent must usually work outside the home, requiring the noncustodial parent to share part of the childcare costs has facilitated employment by more nonaid custodial parents and helped these parents avoid having to apply for welfare. Therefore, when the CSE agency determines the level of a support order, it adds half of the childcare costs into the order. Orders that require the noncustodial parent to share in childcare costs, but do not fix a dollar amount to be paid by the noncustodial parent for childcare are difficult to enforce. It is a prudent practice for a custodial parent to determine the actual costs of childcare, enabling the CSE agency to fix a specified amount.

Child support orders for self-employed noncustodial parents

Determining the ability of a self-employed person to pay child support requires a detailed examination of the person's business income and assets. The self-employed person does not make regular wage reports to a state employment agency, and many do not pay themselves a fixed or regular salary. State and federal tax returns are useful, and are either provided by the parent or obtained from the tax agency. The CSE agency can obtain copies of the noncustodial parent's credit applications and reports as a means of determining his or her true income. The self-employed noncustodial parent may be required to complete a financial statement under penalty of perjury.

The formulas for determining the child support orders are the same as for salaried noncustodial parents, but business expenses and deductions must be considered, and accounting methods that are manipulated to show a paper "loss" or minimal income for a self-employed noncustodial parent who otherwise lives a comfortable life style must be disregarded.

The CSE agency usually deducts "reasonable" out-of-pocket business expenses from the gross income of the self-employed person to arrive at net income that is often higher than that shown on that person's income tax returns. These differences commonly provoke disagreements between the CSE agency and the self-employed parent that require judicial resolution. Self-employed noncustodial parents commonly hire private attorneys to represent them in the resolution of these issues. However, it is possible for a noncustodial parent who operates a small business to resolve these problems without a court hearing.

The net pay of noncustodial parents can also be affected by income from the sale of real estate, from rentals and inheritances, trust account revenues, dividends and returns on stocks and bonds, and interest-bearing accounts. The nonaid custodial parent should provide the agency with as much information as possible on income generating property to enable the agency to make an accurate determination of his or her true income or net worth.

Hardship deductions

In a nonaid case, dependents in the home of the noncustodial parent are his or her legal responsibility and can be credited as hardships that can reduce the amount of support owed. Hardship deductions reduce the amount that the noncustodial parent must pay in child support. However, hardship deductions like these are generally not given in an AFDC case.

There is a dispute as to whether a noncustodial parent is entitled to a hardship deduction for voluntarily supporting a new spouse's children for whom the noncustodial parent is not a biological parent. Some judges give a hardship deduction for voluntary support of stepchildren; others do not. Most agencies do not agree to a hardship deduction for the voluntary support of stepchildren.

A noncustodial parent who has remarried and produced children by his or her new spouse may receive only a 50-percent hardship deduction for the support of the second marriage's children when the new spouse is employed. This is because the new spouse is also responsible for supporting the children of the second marriage and capable of providing that support.

Both custodial and noncustodial parents may claim a hardship deduction to reduce that parent's income for determining the level of a child support order. Many noncustodial parents literally interpret the term "hardship deduction" as if all of their bills and expenses constitute hardships for which they should be given credit. Credit card debt, car payments, mortgage expenses, boat and motorcycle payments, etc., are not considered for purposes of applying the hardship deduction. Many of these expenses are life style choices and any hardship attendant to them has been voluntarily incurred. The law provides that a parent's *first* obligation is the support of his or her child.

The support of a family member who has a life-threatening or catastrophic illness, the support of a dependent parent or grandparent who lives with the parent, the support of one's own biological children from other relationships and for whom no other support is received, and a personal illness that creates financial hardship, are examples of hardships for which the CSE agency normally grants a deduction before determining the child support obligation.

The role of benefits in determining a child support order

A child support order is not calculated only on income from employment. Unemployment Insurance Benefits (UIB), Disability Insurance Benefits (DIB), Worker's Compensation Benefits (WCB), pension or retirement benefits; and Social Security retirement and disability benefits are all considered in determining the level of a child support order, but there are limitations on collection measures against these sources of income. Generally, only 25 percent of these types of benefits can be garnished or attached for child support.

When a noncustodial parent's children are awarded Social Security benefits based on that parent's claim, the amount of the monthly benefits may be credited toward the noncustodial parent's monthly support obligation. If the Social Security payments to the children meet or exceed the noncustodial parent's monthly obligation, he or she is not required to pay any additional monthly support. If the payments fall below the ordered monthly support amount, the noncustodial parent must pay the difference.

When the noncustodial parent is receiving AFDC, or General Assistance, or is unemployed and without income, the agency usually obtains an order in which the determination of the support amount is declared reserved until the parent is able to pay support. This same procedure is followed in calculating reimbursement for AFDC cases. A noncustodial parent who had no income is not required to pay reimbursement for AFDC for that period. In these situations, the court order reserves the establishment of a child support order retroactive to the date that the noncustodial parent becomes able to pay support. A "reserved" child support order simply postpones setting an amount until a later date.

This means that if a noncustodial parent signs a stipulation that reserves support because he or she has no ability to pay it, the agency will not charge any child support at that time but can later establish an order retroactive to the date the noncustodial parent regained the ability to pay support. This process can also be used in nonaid cases. Such orders protect against the noncustodial parent who gains an ability to pay but does not inform the custodial parent or the agency of the change in financial conditions.

Once the agency has determined that the noncustodial parent has the ability to provide support, it may petition the court to set an order for current support that is retroactive to the date that the noncustodial parent became able to pay. This process can create the large amounts of support that commonly face noncustodial parents in cases in which the custodial parent received AFDC. The noncustodial parent who is subject to a reserved order should (and is required to under some orders) notify the agency of a change in financial conditions that would cause the reserved order to be modified to a fixed order.

Support-evasive life styles

Some noncustodial parents appear to live comfortable life styles without having a visible legal means of income. These parents drive new cars, live in upscale homes, wear expensive clothing and jewelry, but claim they have no income from which to pay child support. Some are engaged in illegal activities, and some live off the income or assets of someone else. The CSE agency can request the court to authorize an order of examination, a legal proceeding in which the noncustodial parent is required to answer the questions under oath of a CSE agency attorney regarding sources of income and assets.

Although not without some controversy, it is possible for a judge to order a noncustodial parent who lives off the income and assets of a girlfriend or boyfriend to set a child support order as if the noncustodial parent had income. If the boyfriend or girlfriend acknowledges that he or she supports the noncustodial parent and pays his or her living expenses and debts, the judge can order a child support amount based on the life style enjoyed by the noncustodial parent. The effect of such an order basically forces the new girlfriend or boyfriend to pay the child support obligation on behalf of the noncustodial parent, because the friend has assumed the responsibility to pay all of the other obligations incurred by the noncustodial parent. The friend's only recourse in this situation is to file his or her petition (in the nature of a declaratory relief action) with the court to be relieved of all financial responsibilities previously paid on behalf of the noncustodial parent. Such actions are very rare.

Some noncustodial parents often work "under the table" for cash, and many of them adopt nomadic life styles with no regular employment or fixed place of residence. Obtaining a child support order against these parents is difficult, and collecting is even harder. Their children never receive any support from them; taxpayers become the children's financial parents.

Judges are increasingly issuing "seek work" orders on noncustodial parents who are physically able to work but choose not to. Some judges set child support orders based on the minimum wage the noncustodial parent would earn should that parent become employed, on the theory that ordering payments might motivate these parents to obtain employment and support their children. The agency then must attempt to enforce the child support order and search on a regular basis for assets of the noncustodial parent.

Some states have empowered judges or administrative officers to order a noncustodial parent to attend job training, job placement, vocational rehabilitation, or other work-related programs in an effort to establish or enforce a child support order. Parents should contact their local CSE agencies for more information on the availability of such programs in their areas.

Summary

Society has decided that the first duty of a parent is the support of his or her children. A parent is free to make life style choices for which he or she can pay *after* having provided support for his or her children.

Noncustodial parents need not face financial ruin as the price of supporting their children. Most can pay child support on a regular basis while managing their other financial affairs. The parent who faces financial ruin is the noncustodial parent who runs from his or her obligation and ultimately owes large arrearages and reimbursements for welfare costs. Severe financial enforcement action awaits the child support miscreant.

Chapter 6

Case Management and Enforcement of Child Support Orders

Millions of noncustodial parents do not pay support for their children. As a result, the federal and state governments have enacted and CSE agencies have implemented severe child support enforcement laws. A custodial parent who learns of a change in the financial circumstances of a nonpaying noncustodial parent can notify the agency of the change, as the agency might be able to initiate some of the enforcement remedies we describe in this chapter. Although many actions are automatically implemented by CSE agencies, the agencies need vital information, such as the name of the noncustodial parent's employer, in order to implement these actions.

Wage assignments

Many noncustodial parents do not understand why CSE agencies do not allow them to pay child support directly and voluntarily to the agency, without involving deductions from their wages by their employers. The reason is simple: Many parents do not pay regularly and would not pay at all if the payment process was one of voluntary payments to the agency.

Federal law mandates that all states receiving federal funds for AFDC enact laws requiring that all child support orders contain a wage assignment (or wage garnishment) provision. The enactment of these laws has required CSE agencies to serve court-ordered wage assignments on the employer of every gainfully employed noncustodial parent who has a case with a CSE agency and whose identity can be determined by state-run automated employment records. The only exception to this rule is when the court finds good cause not to require income withholding.

Wage and earnings assignments provide much greater assurance that as long as the noncustodial parent remains employed with an employer on whom a wage assignment order has been served, child support payments will be paid regularly and in a timely fashion. CSE agencies also obtain information from new-hire registries, income tax records, and reports made by the custodial parent, the noncustodial parent, or a former employer of the noncustodial parent.

There are two types of wage assignments: The *standard* wage assignment provides that the same amount is deducted each month from the paycheck of the noncustodial parent and, if applicable, sets a monthly arrears payment.

The *ex parte* wage assignment is a court order that provides that as much as 50 percent of the noncustodial parent's net pay be withheld and sent to the CSE agency each month. It is obtained by the agency ex parte, which means without notice to and without the participation of the nonpaying noncustodial parent. The agency obtains such wage assignments in cases in which the noncustodial parent owes a large arrearage and does not comply with the order.

In states that operate under administrative process instead of judicial process, the CSE agency is allowed to directly issue a Notice of Assignment without requesting that a court issue the Earnings Assignment Order. The Notice of Assignment has the same effect as a judge-issued Earnings Assignment Order. When the agency inherits an existing child support order or wage assignment payable to the custodial parent, it must usually intervene in the case that produced the order. A Motion for Intervention or similar legal document is filed, in which the CSE agency petitions the court to allow it to intervene and order that all future payments be redirected to the agency instead of the custodial parent.

The agency can also obtain a wage assignment authorizing the withholding of up to 50 percent of the noncustodial parent's monthly income when forced to establish an order by default judgment. If the noncustodial parent whose employer has been served with a 50-percent wage assignment order contacts the agency to request that a lesser monthly payment be set on the arrears, the agency often agrees to stipulate to a regular wage assignment. However, if the noncustodial parent owes a large arrearage and has a poor payment history, the agency might refuse the request, forcing the noncustodial parent to apply to the court for modification.

Once a wage assignment is served on the noncustodial parent's employer, the employer is required by law to withhold the amount stated and forward it to the agency at regular intervals based on the employer's pay periods. As a result of the Welfare Reform Act, the employer will be required to send the support no later than seven days from the date it was withheld from the paycheck.

An employer who fails to comply can be made to pay to the CSE agency the amount of the child support order that was not withheld. Employers are also subject to penalties and fines ranging from $500 to $1,000 (depending on state law). An employer may not refuse employment to, discharge, or take disciplinary action against a noncustodial parent who is subject to income withholding, but may charge the employee a fee for processing the wage assignment.

Multiple orders assigning wages are often served on a noncustodial parent's employer when the parent has other children for whom he or she has a child support order, or when he or she owes back taxes or other debts. In these situations, the total amount ordered withheld usually exceeds the maximum allowable withholding of 50 percent, and can even exceed the parent's total income. When multiple wage assignments have been served, the employer may not withhold more than 50 percent of that employee's net income. If the amount withheld by the employer is less than the child support amount that is owed each month, the CSE agency may use other collection procedures to collect the remaining amount due. Any unpaid amount accrues as child support arrears.

The basic rule on priority of wage assignments is that current child support is always paid first. However, when the noncustodial parent's employer is served with more than one wage assignment for current child support, some states permit the employer to divide the withheld wages into equal amounts, not to exceed the amount stated in the assignment for current support. Other states require employers to honor wage assignments for current support based on the sequence in which they were served on the employer.

After the employer has honored all of the wage assignments for current child support, any balance remaining in the withheld wages is applied to arrearages and other withholding orders that have been served on the employer. Most state laws require employers to notify the agency when the noncustodial parent terminates employment and provide the name of the noncustodial parent's new employer, if known.

Wages, salary, military allotments, some vacation trust accounts, severance pay, sick pay, incentive pay, commissions, bonuses, income from interest-bearing accounts, annuities, survivor's benefits, worker's compensation benefits, pensions, retirement, Social Security retirement, and Social Security disability benefits are all subject to wage or earnings assignment orders.

When children receive lump sum (retroactive) Social Security benefits based on the noncustodial parent's disability claim, the lump sum is usually credited toward arrearages. The Social Security Administration generally establishes the period of time for which the benefits are issued. If this period coincides with the period for which arrearages are owed, the benefits may often be credited against those arrearages.

Some sources of income—Unemployment Insurance Benefits (UIB), State Disability Insurance Benefits (DIB), and lottery winnings—are subject to automatic withholding pursuant to state law and do not require a wage assignment. These kinds of income are intercepted at the state agency that pays the benefits, and the moneys are diverted to the CSE agency. In California, 25 percent of state UIB and DIB can be intercepted, while 100 percent of lottery winnings are subject to intercept. In situations in which 25 percent of unemployment or disability insurance benefits exceeds the amount of monthly child support owed, the noncustodial parent can request that the agency adjust the percentage of the unemployment or disability insurance benefits withheld, so the withheld amount equals the monthly support obligation.

Noncustodial parents who are employed in "seasonal" jobs are advised to put aside into a savings account enough money to make up any child support deficiency during periods of unemployment. Doing so will ensure against becoming delinquent if unemployment benefits fall short of the full monthly obligation owed.

The agency serves health insurance orders on the employer of a noncustodial parent who has failed to provide health insurance for his or her children. If coverage is not available through the noncustodial parent's employer, the employer who has been served the assignment must notify the agency. The noncustodial parent employee must complete the appropriate enrollment forms required to implement the insurance, and the employer may charge the noncustodial parent with the additional monthly premium for the children's health insurance. The employer must initiate coverage for the children within 30 days after the health insurance order has been served on the employer; the employer is not required to wait until the open enrollment period that otherwise regulates additions or changes to an employee's health plan. If dental and vision coverage is part of the plan, it must also be provided. An employer who willfully fails to comply with a health insurance order can be cited for contempt of court.

Self-employed noncustodial parents can be served with wage assignment orders that in effect require them to withhold their own wages. Most do not comply with wage assignments orders on their own wages.

Partly because of this difficulty, California became the first state to implement the State Licensing Match System (SLMS). Many self-employed people—such as doctors, lawyers, real estate agents, commercial truck drivers, nurses, and contractors—must obtain a professional license issued by the state or a state-regulated agency that enables them to work in their professions. The California SLMS works very much like a blacklist. The system matches a state-generated list of noncustodial parents whose cases are handled by CSE agencies and who are not complying with their child support orders, with the lists of applicants for state-issued licenses. If the licensing agency matches the name of a nonpaying noncustodial parent with the name on an application for issuance or renewal of a license, it denies or defers approval of the application until the noncustodial parent takes action to remove his or her name from the list. SLMS forces noncustodial parents to pay their delinquent support or face losing their professional licenses until they comply with the court-ordered child support.

As initially drafted in California, the SLMS bill covered all driver's, hunting, and fishing licenses. The bill was amended to delete these from the list of licenses whose issuance or renewal was subject to intercept for nonpayment of child support. However, the Welfare Reform Act requires states to include *all* regular driver's licenses, professional licenses, and recreational licenses in the category of licenses that can be withheld for nonpayment of child support.

The California SLMS has been so successful that other states have enacted their own license intercept and suspension system. Failure to comply with subpoenas or warrants relating to establishing paternity or child support can also result in suspension of all such licenses.

The Welfare Reform Act also requires states to provide lists to the federal government of persons owing more than $5,000 in child support arrearages. The names of nonpaying noncustodial parents are to be reported to the U.S. State Department, which will revoke, restrict, or limit the passports previously issued to the people on these lists.

Child support arrearages

In addition to the enforcement tools used by CSE agencies to collect current child support, agencies also target the collection of child support arrearages.

State and Federal Tax Intercept Program

The most widely known enforcement tool for CSE agencies to collect child support arrearages is the State and Federal Tax Intercept Program. Any case handled by an agency in which child support or spousal support arrearages are owed, even those cases in which the noncustodial parent is already making payments pursuant to a court-ordered payment schedule, is covered by the tax intercept program. However, nonaid cases in which current support is no longer an issue (the children have become adults) are not submitted for tax intercept.

Every year all CSE agencies submit to state and federal governments a list of cases in which the noncustodial parent has a support arrearage and the amount of the arrearage. The IRS and state income tax agencies match the names (using Social Security numbers) with that tax agency's records of taxpayers to whom refunds are to be paid. Any tax refund owed to someone whose name appears on these lists is paid instead to the agency that submitted the name, as long as the amount owed in support arrearages exceeds $500, and as long as the amount intercepted does not exceed the amount owed. Tax refund intercepts may be used only to pay child or spousal support arrearages; they may not be given to the CSE agency for the payment of a current child support obligation.

The noncustodial parent whose name is submitted for tax refund intercept is notified by the IRS and/or state income tax agency of the submission of his or her name. The notice reflects the amount of back child support claimed, and the name and address of the agency that submitted the name for intercept. When the agency receives an income tax refund intercept that appears to pay all of the support arrearages, it audits the case to ensure that the amounts claimed are correct. When the audit discloses that additional amounts such as interest are owed, or arrearages are owed in another case handled by the agency or another jurisdiction, tax intercept refunds are applied to these debts. Any tax intercept refunds that exceed the amount owed by the noncustodial parent are refunded.

If the spouse of a noncustodial parent has his or her portion of an income tax refund intercepted because of the noncustodial parent's arrearages, he or she must contact the IRS or state tax agency to determine the process for contesting the amount. The tax agency provides instructions for filing a claim for a return of the spouse's portion of the tax refund intercepted. The spouse of a noncustodial parent should *not* contact the CSE agency to contest the amount of the intercept.

President Clinton signed new federal legislation in conjunction with the Welfare Reform Act, called the Federal Debt Collection Act. This was created to enable the government to collect debts that are not tax related, and includes the power for CSE agencies to collect arrearages. CSE agencies will be able to intercept any payments a delinquent noncustodial parent may receive from the federal government without using a wage assignment. It is similar to state and federal tax return, UIB, and DIB intercepts.

Federal employees' paychecks and pension benefits will be intercepted automatically when the noncustodial parent receiving these funds is found delinquent in his or her support. The Department of the Treasury Financial Management Service (FMS) and the Office of

Child Support Enforcement (OCSE) have begun implementing this executive order and the program will be phased in gradually. FMS intercept letters have begun to be mailed out advising parents that they are subject to funds intercept. Contact your CSE agency for more information on this new program.

Many CSE agencies work closely with their state's income tax collection agency to locate the assets and earnings of noncustodial parents. Although state taxing authorities often do not wield any greater legal powers than those used by CSE agencies, they often can use highly automated computer systems to immediately access asset information and act to seize these assets more quickly than CSE agencies. State taxing authorities receive federal funding when they assist CSE agencies in collecting child support. CSE agencies usually submit to the state taxing authorities the cases on which they have had the greatest difficulty in collection. When the state's tax collection authority and the CSE agency take overlapping enforcement action, one agency is required to stop and allow the other agency to continue the enforcement actions.

Credit

When a noncustodial parent is more than two months delinquent in his or her child support obligation, the CSE agency is required by law to submit that parent's name, the amount owed, and the payment history on the arrearage to credit reporting agencies.

When a delinquent noncustodial parent whose name has been reported to credit reporting agencies attempts to obtain a loan, or otherwise applies for credit, that parent's support payment history is displayed for the business or agency to whom the credit application has been submitted.

Credit reporting helps prevent noncustodial parents from incurring new debts that might cause them to be unable to pay existing obligations. A noncustodial parent who has a credit report showing nonpayment of child support is unlikely to be approved for credit for the purchase of a car, a home loan, or the issuance or credit line increase of a credit card.

A noncustodial parent who believes that information submitted to the credit reporting bureau is inaccurate must file a consumer's dispute with the credit bureau—not the CSE agency. The credit reporting bureau then notifies the agency of the dispute and requests that the agency verify the information. The agency must correct any inaccurate reports, but if the agency believes its report was correct, it advises the credit reporting agencies of the verification.

The three most prominent credit reporting bureaus to which CSE agencies report credit information are Trans Union, Equifax, and TRW. Because CSE agencies usually report their information to all three agencies, a noncustodial parent who disputes the accuracy of information reported by a CSE agency should file a dispute over the credit information with all three credit reporting agencies.

Property liens

Many CSE agencies record their child support orders with the Office of the Recorder in the county in which the CSE agency believes the obligor may own real estate. Some agencies record a child support order only when the noncustodial parent becomes delinquent in paying pursuant to the order. The legal effect of recording an order is that a lien is placed on all real property owned by the obligor in the county or jurisdiction in which the judgment is recorded. The lien prevents the delinquent noncustodial parent from selling, refinancing, or transferring title to the real estate without first paying the arrearages.

When the noncustodial parent sells real estate or refinances an existing real estate loan subject to a property lien, the escrow company sends the seller's proceeds of the sale to the CSE agency, up to the amount of the unpaid child or spousal support arrearages owed. The existence of a lien on a piece of real estate causes many lenders to disapprove an application for a home improvement loan or an application for a loan secured with a second deed of trust until the obligation has been satisfied, because child support liens take priority over all other liens, except those held by the first mortgage holder.

CSE agencies can file liens against other assets of a delinquent noncustodial parent—worker's compensation settlements and judgments in civil lawsuits—that are not subject to wage withholding. Because the agency is often unaware of possible or pending judgments in favor of an obligor, the custodial parent should report the details surrounding that lawsuit to the CSE agency. The most beneficial information a custodial parent can provide about a pending civil action involving the noncustodial parent is the name of the court in which the lawsuit has been filed and the docket or case number assigned to the suit. A custodial parent who notifies the agency of a worker's compensation lawsuit should also report the name of the employer involved in the action.

Once the agency learns of the worker's compensation action or civil lawsuit, it files a lien with the clerk of the court or board before which the action is pending. This ensures that before moneys are paid to the noncustodial parent as part of a civil judgment or worker's compensation settlement or judgment, the amount claimed for unpaid support is paid to the agency. If the amount of the worker's compensation settlement, judgment, or civil judgment exceeds the amount of the child support lien, the noncustodial parent receives the funds that remain after the lien has been paid.

Writ of execution

Another enforcement action used by CSE agencies to collect delinquent and unpaid child support is the writ of execution, commonly known as a bank levy because writs of execution are frequently used against bank accounts. A writ of execution is an order issued and signed by a judge that may be served on the institution or person holding the funds to be seized. They are commonly served by the local sheriff; to freeze the assets to be seized. The assets may not be released to the noncustodial parent obligor or transferred to any other person without the prior approval of the court issuing the writ. Writs of execution may be levied against a variety of assets including checking and savings accounts, funds held in the noncustodial parent's place of business (such as the cash register), funds held in vacation or other trust accounts, and property for which the noncustodial parent is a named beneficiary in an inheritance.

The noncustodial parent is normally allowed by law a specified period of time, usually described in the instructions on the writ of execution, to contest the issuance of the writ. The court that issued a writ may terminate or modify it on the application of the noncustodial parent if good cause is shown. However, if the court declines to modify or recall the writ, when the time allowed to contest it has expired assets subject to seizure are sent to the sheriff for delivery to the CSE agency. The agency then credits the funds to the unpaid support arrearages.

Custodial parents can assist a CSE by determining the location of the noncustodial parent's bank accounts and other assets. From a check the custodial parent can obtain the name of the bank, the branch location, and the account number of noncustodial parent's account. A custodial parent not sure where to find this information should give a photocopy of the check to the agency. The custodial parent should relay to the CSE agency all information concerning the noncustodial parent's accounts, to enable the CSE to obtain a writ of execution on these accounts.

The same advice applies to information about possible a inheritance. A custodial parent frequently learns of deaths in the family of the noncustodial parent, because the information appears in local newspapers and because the children frequently tell the custodial parent.

A common problem for CSE agencies has been that financial information on bank and savings accounts has been considered confidential, and many states have enacted laws to protect account holders from unauthorized release of financial information. The Welfare Reform Act requires every state to develop a data match system for quarterly exchange of information. Financial institutions will be required to provide to the states the names, addresses, Social Security numbers, and any other identifying information on all noncustodial parents who maintain accounts and owe past-due child support. Financial institutions will not be held liable for disclosing this information to CSE agencies or for honoring the levy or writ of execution on a parent's bank account. Until a state has implemented a data match system with financial institutions in that state, a custodial parent should continue to provide this information to the CSE agency.

The custodial parent should immediately notify the CSE agency of the death of the noncustodial parent. Most CSE agencies require proof of the death—a death certificate, newspaper article, or obituary. The death terminates the current support obligation, but the custodial parent may be able to apply for Social Security Survivor benefits on behalf of the children.

In addition, the estate of the deceased parent sometimes contains assets against which the CSE agency can file a lien. Because the estate of the deceased noncustodial parent can sometimes be seized to satisfy an unpaid child support debt, a custodial parent to whom unpaid child support is owed should provide the agency with the name and location of the court, the name of the probate officer, and the docket or probate case number, to enable the CSE agency to file a lien against the estate.

Bankruptcy

Some noncustodial parents believe they can discharge their child support obligations for current child support and arrearages by filing for bankruptcy. Under federal bankruptcy laws, child support obligations are not discharged by bankruptcy of the parent who owes child support. Previously, some noncustodial parent successfully discharged child support reimbursement owed on welfare cases. The Welfare Reform Act has eliminated this loophole in the bankruptcy law. Now, no portion of any child support-related debt is dischargeable.

The federal bankruptcy statute provides different kinds of bankruptcies, known by the number of the chapter of the statute in which they are described. We will examine the two most common types:

A Chapter 7 bankruptcy seeks the discharge of all debts. Prior to the Welfare Reform Act, CSE agencies were required to respond to Chapter 7 filings by noncustodial parents by filing a petition with the bankruptcy court; the petition sought to protect against the discharge of child support arrearages. The Welfare Reform Act has eliminated the need for an agency to file a petition. However, CSE agencies must stop their efforts to collect child support arrearages that built up *prior* to the date the noncustodial parent filed the Chapter 7 bankruptcy until it has been discharged. Then a CSE agency may renew its collection efforts.

In a Chapter 13 bankruptcy, the debtor seeks temporary relief from his or her creditors and seeks to set up a payment plan in which the creditors each receive a portion of the debtor's assets. During the first 90 days from the date of the filing of the petition, all creditors, including CSE agencies, must stop efforts to collect arrearages owed by the bankrupt person. CSE agencies terminate the mailing of a monthly statement to the noncustodial parent and any wage assignment that has been served on the parent's employer. However, because current child support is not included in the automatic stay on collection efforts, the CSE agency may continue its efforts to collect current child support. This means a wage assignment for current child support can be continued.

A Chapter 13 bankruptcy is supervised by a trustee who determines the assets of the bankrupt noncustodial parent and creates a payment plan based on these assets, which normally include property, wages, and tax refunds due to the noncustodial parent. If the trustee includes projected income tax refunds, the agency must remove the tax intercept flag and is precluded from intercepting the parent's tax refunds. However, if the tax refund is not listed in the Chapter 13 bankruptcy, or if it had already been intercepted when bankruptcy was filed, the agency may keep it. Any tax refunds intercepted after they have been listed in the bankruptcy plan must be turned over to the Chapter 13 trustee, as these funds are considered part of the bankruptcy assets to be divided among the creditors listed in the plan.

After the plan has been confirmed by the court, the CSE agency is free to attempt to collect any arrearages that occur after the date of the filing of the petition. Support arrearages that occurred before the filing of the petition are subject to the terms of the plan. Once the Chapter 13 bankruptcy has been finally discharged, the agency may resume normal efforts to collect arrearages that occurred prior to the bankruptcy.

Account audits and interest

Most complaints that are made to CSE agencies come from parents who feel that their balances are incorrect. Sometimes the custodial parent feels that the account balance is lower than what the noncustodial parent actually owes; sometimes the noncustodial parent believes the account is overstated. These parents frequently request that their accounts be audited. Most agencies do not perform an audit unless the requesting parent provides good reason. Because CSE agencies monitor thousands of accounts, and some operate without computer systems, an audit may not be the highest priority of the CSE agency. For example, an audit necessary to satisfy a property lien would likely be performed before a discretionary audit to resolve a dispute over the amount owed.

Frequent audits and frequent changes made to an account—the custodial parent starts and terminates from welfare, children move back and forth between the parents, children emancipate without anyone notifying the agency—commonly cause discrepancies in an account.

To assist parents in monitoring their accounts, we have provided a form in Chapter 11. Every custodial and noncustodial parent should keep a record of the amounts owed and the amounts that have been paid. Noncustodial parents should keep copies of their pay stubs that itemize child support payments by wage assignment, canceled checks used to pay direct child support, and receipts for support paid by money orders. The noncustodial parent is wise to keep a record of all payments until the last child has emancipated, all arrearages have been paid in full, and the agency has given notification that the case will be closed.

CSE agencies audit child support accounts when a title company requests confirmation of the amount owed, when the child support case is scheduled for a court hearing, when intercepted income tax refund money is received, or when either the custodial or noncustodial parent presents a legitimate reason for an audit. The process of determining the correct amount owed begins with a review of the terms of the court order.

For example, if the court order sets child support at $500 per month effective January 1, 1996, and fixes welfare reimbursement or arrearages at $2,500 for the period of January 1, 1995, through December 31, 1995, the auditor computes the total amount that should have been paid under the order at $2,500 plus $500 per month from January 1, 1996, to the date of the audit.

After determining the total amount that should have been paid, the auditor credits each payment to the month it was made or when the moneys were withheld from the parent's wages. The date of receipt of a payment is commonly called the legal date of collection. If payment was dated or withheld on May 20, 1996, but not posted to the account until June 5, 1996, the payment is credited as a payment of current support for May of 1996, not June of 1996. Tax intercepts, however, are credited to the account in the month in which the intercepted funds were received by the CSE agency.

Many factors affect monthly current child support. If the children live with the noncustodial parent for more than a few days—30 consecutive days is typical—the noncustodial parent's duty to pay child support during the period is abated. However, if the children visit for only a few days or weeks, the visit is treated as normal visitation, and does not affect support payments. When the custodial parent stops receiving welfare, the account is adjusted so that payments go to the custodial parent and not the welfare department. When a child emancipates, the agency adjusts the account to stop charging the non-custodial parent for current child support and adjusts the schedule to cover arrearages. When there are multiple children, adjusting the current child support order is easy when the court order is a "per child" order, because the amount expected is reduced by the amount attributable to the emancipated child.

However, if the court order for multiple children contains a lump sum figure for current support covering all of the children, the emancipation of one does not automatically reduce the amount of current support. The amount due is reduced only if the parent applies for a modification of the order, and is terminated only by court order or the emancipation of all children covered by the order. When a child covered by a current support order that is not a "per child" order goes to live with the noncustodial parent or emancipates, the noncustodial parent should request the agency review the case for modification.

The CSE agency credits payments received in a given month (except for tax intercepts and funds received from a lien or writ of execution) first to the noncustodial parent's current support obligation. If payments received in a given month exceed the amount due for current support, the excess amounts are applied to arrearages. If the noncustodial parent does not owe arrearages, excess payments are refunded, and the wage assignment on the parent's earnings should be adjusted so that only the amount due in current support is withheld. This procedure produces a final balance owed by the noncustodial parent. A parent whose records do not agree with the audit of the agency is able to compare his or her records with the case audit to locate the discrepancy.

Many CSE agencies charge interest on unpaid child support. These charges are usually shown on monthly statements as a lump sum addition or regular monthly charge. Fully automated agencies list the principal balance and interest charged on monthly statements. CSE agencies not yet automated calculate the interest charges separately at the time of an account audit and add these interest charges to the account in a lump sum.

Parents not aware of the impact of interest are frequently astonished at the speed with which it can increase the amount owed on arrearages. Noncustodial parents who owe arrearages should know that the interest charged is the same as many other credit accounts. In California, the interest rate on arrearages is 10 percent per year. The effect of interest should be a real incentive for noncustodial parents to avoid delinquencies in payments and to pay off accounts containing arrearages.

> *Our CSE agency handled a case of a noncustodial parent who accrued a welfare-reimbursement obligation from 1979 to 1986, before he gained custody of the child. Even though the current support order was $100 per month, he never paid any current child support during this period. In 1994 our agency received a request from a title company to provide them with a payoff balance on the account, because the noncustodial parent wanted to refinance his home. The noncustodial parent assumed he owed only the $9,600 in principal ($100 per month times 96 months) he failed to pay from 1979 to 1986. He decided he could afford to pay $9,600 from the equity he would receive on the refinancing of his home. However, the audit of the account added interest to the account balance, and the total balance due was more than $20,000.*

Here is another case history illustrating the impact of interest on noncustodial parents who don't pay their child support as ordered:

> *The order for monthly child support was $150 per month ($50 per child for three children) effective October 1, 1975. The only support paid was received through tax refund intercepts. When this noncustodial parent's case was audited on December 31, 1996, he owed a principal balance of $5,814.48 in back support. But 21 years of interest on the unpaid child support increased the amount owed by this noncustodial parent to $24,135.44—a 21-year loan at 10 percent interest.*

The following list shows which states have implemented laws governing interest charges, whether or not the states are currently charging interest (as of July 1, 1997), and their rates. States that do not charge interest will begin to charge interest when they obtain systems that will allow them to calculate it.

States whose statutes allow CSE agencies to charge interest, but not currently charging interest:

Arkansas	10%	North Dakota	12%
Iowa	10%	Nevada	12%
Idaho	10.875%	New Hampshire	6%
Illinois	9%	New Jersey	N/A
Indiana	1.5% per mo.	Oklahoma	10%
Kentucky	Legal rate	Oregon	9%
Louisiana	9.75%	Pennsylvania	6%
Maine	6%	South Dakota	1% per mo.
Massachusetts	Not yet set	Utah	N/A
Michigan*	8% semi-annum	Vermont	12%
Minnesota	Current rate +2%	Washington	12%
Mississippi	8%	Wyoming	N/A
Missouri	1%		
Montana	10%		
North Carolina	10%		

*Michigan's rate is a surcharge and is not called interest.

N/A= Not available

States currently charging interest:

Alabama	12%	New York	9%
Alaska	12%	Rhode Island	1% per mo.
Arizona	10%	South Carolina	14%
California	10%	Tennessee	12%
Colorado	Varies by county	Texas	12%
Kansas	10%	Virginia	9%
Nebraska	Court decides	West Virginia	10%
New Mexico	8.75%	Wisconsin	1.5%

States not under statute and not currently charging interest:

Connecticut	Georgia	Maryland
Delaware	Hawaii	Ohio
Florida		

All of the interest rates listed are annual rates, except as otherwise noted. Contact your CSE agency to verify the effect of interest on your case, because some states may have changed their laws after July 1, 1997.

Legal consequences and remedies for failure to pay

Many CSE agencies have created special units staffed by field investigators and special prosecutors to handle cases in which the CSE seeks civil contempt against and criminal prosecutions of nonpaying noncustodial parents. A noncustodial parent who has the ability to pay child support but refuses to voluntarily pay and attempts to hide assets, can be criminally charged with a misdemeanor.

If a delinquent noncustodial parent continues to avoid payment after a misdemeanor prosecution, the agency can request the court to find the nonpaying parent in contempt of court. If after a contempt of court conviction the noncustodial parent still does not pay, he or she can be criminally charged with willful failure to support a child, which in many jurisdictions can be prosecuted as a felony.

Since nonpaying noncustodial parents do not pay child support, their incarceration does not impede payment of support. Contempt proceedings might motivate them to produce the funds required to escape incarceration, and can serve as a deterrent to other nonpaying parents. Many agencies now actively use contempt and criminal prosecutions.

Some states have enacted laws to detect and deter fraudulent transfers of property by noncustodial parents who attempt to hide their assets. The Welfare Reform Act requires states to enact laws to enable CSE agencies to seek court orders that void transfers of property by noncustodial parents who attempt to escape paying support. Laws such as the Uniform Fraudulent Conveyance Act prohibit the transfer of assets owned by a debtor to another individual in order to avoid a child support obligation. States are required to void such fraudulent transactions or obtain settlements with noncustodial parents that are in the best interests of the children.

Courts confronted by noncustodial parents who claim they are unemployed and/or have no assets from which to pay support have the power to order these parents to seek and obtain employment—an action known as a "seek-work" order. Courts also have the power to order noncustodial parents who claim they have no assets or employment to devise a plan approved by the court to satisfy the delinquent obligation. As long as the noncustodial parent is not physically or mentally incapacitated, the court can order him or her to find a job and present to the court or CSE agency logs proving active pursuit of employment.

Courts have the power to require a noncustodial parent who has been found in contempt to post a bond as insurance against that parent's failure to honor the order and to prevent the parent from leaving the state. Posting a compliance bond is often ordered instead of incarceration. A parent who has posted a bond and fails to honor the payment plan approved by the court forfeits the bond and is subject to arrest and incarceration.

CSE agencies also have the power, with the assistance of the IRS and state income tax agencies, to seize the assets of a nonpaying noncustodial parent. Some states now authorize CSE agencies to use administrative writs of execution that bypass the state tax agencies. CSE agencies then seize assets without court orders by issuing an administrative writ. Noncustodial parents who continually fail to honor their court orders for child support can lose their homes, cars, boats, property, jewelry, and other personal property that is subject to seizure and sale at auction. Asset seizure has been an underutilized enforcement tool, because the amount of work necessary to seize assets makes this remedy less effective in an agency handling thousands of child support cases. The advent of sophisticated computer systems operated by CSE agencies might result in a substantial increase in asset seizures in the future.

Not every CSE agency in the United States uses all of the enforcement measures described in this chapter. Nor does every child support case justify all of these actions; more extreme enforcement procedures are reserved for the more extreme cases of nonpayment. A custodial parent unsure of the enforcement procedures used by the agency handling his or her case should talk to the agency staff.

Deadbeats—you can run but you can't hide

The term "deadbeat" is used by some child support enforcement professionals to describe parents who are capable of paying child support but refuse to do so. Although the term is not found in the standard vocabulary of CSE agencies, the term is commonly used by the news media to describe sensational cases of nonsupport. Many CSE agencies have implemented "wanted" posters for the purpose of publicly stigmatizing child support "deadbeats" and encouraging citizens to help locate these parents and their assets.

112

Our CSE agency was one of the first agencies to produce a television show on "deadbeat" parents. This show was broadcast on a public access channel and was highly publicized. We used this show to broadcast the names, pictures, and arrears balances of the worst non-paying offenders in our agency's caseload. One of the results of this program was the voluntary payment of arrearages by embarrassed noncustodial parents who wanted to ensure their cases would not be broadcast. Other agencies have utilized this idea as well.

The following two true-life stories illustrate some of the foolish efforts that some noncustodial parents make to avoid paying child support. The names of the parents have been withheld.

The noncustodial father is a commercial fisherman who operates his own fishing boat and lives in Massachusetts with his second wife. The custodial mother lives in California with their one child, who is now emancipated. The parents divorced in 1976, and the father was ordered to pay $250 per month in child support. Because he lived out-of-state and was self-employed, he was able to avoid paying his obligation for many years.

The custodial mother opened a case with the CSE agency in California. The agency initiated an interstate action, requesting Massachusetts to search for assets belonging to the father and collect current child support and arrearages of $41,000. Because Massachusetts does not collect interest on child support cases, interest was not added to the balance. The Massachusetts child support enforcement caseworker brought the father into a Massachusetts court to answer to charges of failure to pay. After a long court battle, the father eventually produced documents showing that he had just been divorced from his second wife, and lost his business, home, and all his assets to her. The father claimed he would never be able to pay his support arrearages, and he offered to settle by paying $7,000.

The father's attorney told the mother that she could accept the $7,000 settlement or receive nothing. The mother accepted the $7,000, which was the first child support payment she had received in many years.

When advised of the settlement the California agency closed the case, but the Massachusetts caseworker felt that something was "fishy." She monitored the activities of the father and discovered that the father and his second wife remarried. All the assets the father claimed he had lost in the divorce reverted back to his name.

The noncustodial father had created a sham divorce with fraudulent transfer of his assets to his second wife as part of the settlement, in order to escape his support obligation. After the father and his second wife decided they had waited an appropriate length of time, they remarried.

The Massachusetts caseworker reopened the case and requested that California reopen its case. The Massachusetts caseworker requested that the Massachusetts court set aside its previous judgment approving the $7,000 settlement. The court granted the caseworker's request and reinstated the entire remaining arrearage of $34,000 as a new judgment against the father. The Massachusetts court ordered the father to make monthly payments of $150 on the arrearage. Several months later, the father and his second wife attempted to refinance their home. The Massachusetts agency had filed a lien on their home and collected the entire $34,000 arrearage from the proceeds of the escrow account. The custodial mother received the $34,000 in January of 1997 and is using the money to finance her child's college education.

A physician and his former wife had three children (now adults) and were divorced in Texas in 1982. The father, an obstetrician/gynecologist, was ordered to pay $600 per month in child support as part of his divorce judgment. The father never voluntarily paid support, and moved to California. In 1985 the mother, who did not know of the father's move, also moved to California. After numerous unsuccessful attempts to locate the father, the mother opened a child support case with the CSE agency.

The agency located the noncustodial father living in California. The CSE brought the father to court, and after a year of hearings, the court found him in contempt for failure to comply with the order. The California court fixed the arrears at $68,000, and ordered that he be confined in the county jail. The *court then suspended the father's sentence to enable him to pay arrearages through wage assignment where he worked. The father made four payments by wage assignment before terminating his employment with the hospital and moving to New York.*

The California agency initiated an interstate action to New York. New York reduced the father's arrearages to $12,000 because of the state's statute of limitations on judgments, and the New York court ordered the father to pay his support by wage assignment where he was employed. After only four payments, the father again quit his employment and moved to Kansas, where he set up a private practice. The California agency initiated another interstate action, this time with Kansas. The agency in Kansas filed a contempt action against the noncustodial father.

The California agency asked the Kansas agency to throw the book at the father, as they believed the father was crossing state lines to avoid paying child support. The father hired another attorney to fight the Kansas action. After a two-year effort in which the father attempted to capitalize on Kansas's statute of limitations, the father claimed that the publicity his case had caused him to lose all his patients and prevented him from finding a job. The father claimed that his family-friend bookkeeper had absconded with all of his money, although no police report or charges had ever been filed.

This time the Kansas court ruled that the noncustodial father owed the full amount of support that had been claimed by California. However, the father hid his assets, and the court fixed a payment schedule of $300 per month on the case that had become an arrears-only case due to the emancipation of all three children. Kansas collects interest on child support arrearages, and the Kansas court fixed the principal and interest on the arrearages at $172,000. The court sentenced the father to serve six months in jail to begin when he missed his first payment on the arrearages. The father made three payments in Kansas, then stopped again and moved to Wisconsin.

The custodial mother in California is still waiting to collect back child support, and California has once again filed an interstate action, this time with Wisconsin. California has requested that an action be filed in the federal courts against the father for interstate flight to avoid payment. We expect the father to repeat his pattern of courtroom litigation followed by flight to another state.

The case of this noncustodial parent is representative of thousands of cases handled by CSE agencies. We are hard-pressed to understand why some parents choose to pay thousands of dollars in interest, attorney fees, and other expenses to avoid child support instead of paying the amounts of child support owed. When these noncustodial parents retire and expect to receive retirement income, they might discover that their Social Security checks and pension payments are reduced, because the agency has followed them into retirement.

Chapter 7

Modifying an Existing Child Support Order

Because child support orders commonly last for many years, it is expected that the physical and financial circumstances of both parents and the children will change. Arrangements between the parents for the custody change; sometimes a parent loses or changes employment or becomes disabled, and occasionally, the financial condition of one parent improves dramatically. All of these circumstances can justify a change in the child support order.

Unfortunately, many parents involved in child support cases do not know it is possible to have their child support orders modified to reflect these changes. Far too many custodial parents live with outdated orders that do not reflect the substantial improvement in the ability of the noncustodial parent to pay child support. Far too many noncustodial parents who have lost their employment, become incarcerated or disabled, or become otherwise unable to pay the child support that was originally ordered, have never obtained modifications of their support orders. These noncustodial parents, who have either neglected to request a modification or who have not known of their right to request one, have accumulated staggering amounts of arrearages that should not have accrued, because they were unable to pay the amount that was ordered.

A parent whose current child support order is at least three years old, who experiences a change in circumstances, or who becomes aware of a change of circumstances in the other parent's life that might cause a beneficial modification of the support order, should call or write the CSE agency to request a formal modification review.

Prior to 1988, modifications of child support orders handled by CSE agencies were conducted on a sporadic case-by-case basis. In 1988 Congress enacted a law that requires all CSE agencies to review the support order in every AFDC case to see if a modification is justified. The result of this law was that thousands of outdated orders were modified to bring the level of support into line with present-day costs of living and current child support guidelines.

The standard time for a CSE agency to conduct a modification review of a child support order is every three years, but a parent who believes his or her personal situation or the circumstances of the other parent have changed may request a modification review without waiting the three-year period. The agency conducts a modification review, usually without any charge to either parent, and handles all of the paperwork attendant to the review. However, some states do charge a reasonable fee for modifications.

Once a review is requested, the agency is obliged to modify the order without regard to which parent has requested it. A modification review can produce a result very different than expected by the parent who requested the review. For example, if the noncustodial parent has requested a review thinking that the amount of child support should be reduced, and the review shows that the amount should be increased, the CSE must move to increase the amount. Likewise, a custodial parent who requests a review in the belief that the order will be increased can find the level of child support decreased. Occasionally, the review determines that a modification is not warranted, and the existing judgment remains in effect.

Financial errors of the noncustodial parent

Many noncustodial parents become financially unable to comply with a child support order when they are incarcerated. Some incarcerated noncustodial parents do not care about their child support orders; other incarcerated noncustodial parents do care about their child support orders, but mistakenly believe that their incarceration automatically reduces or abates their duty to provide child support, without the need to obtain a court order terminating or reducing the obligation while they are incarcerated. No change of circumstance abates, reduces, or increases a court order for child support unless another court order changes the first one.

The incarcerated noncustodial parent who ignores the child support order or believes that no action is needed to modify the order based on his or her incarceration discovers too late (usually when he or she becomes reemployed after release from incarceration) that child support arrearages accumulated during the incarceration. Arrearages that have accumulated *cannot* be erased, even when the noncustodial parent presents evidence that shows his or her incarceration constituted a lack of ability to comply with the support order. These parents frequently find that their reemployment is accompanied by a 50 percent garnishment of their paychecks to liquidate the arrearages they accumulated while in custody. It is not uncommon for incarcerated noncustodial parents to accumulate arrearages of $25,000 or more because they failed to seek a modification of the order. That oversight can become financially devastating to the noncustodial parent upon release.

This same situation occurs when noncustodial parents have lost their employment and their incomes. Unless these parents petition the court for a modification of the order to reflect their reduced earnings and reduced abilities to pay, their arrearages accumulate and they can be labeled as "deadbeats."

Occasionally, the CSE agency obtains a support order by a default judgment, because it does not know the noncustodial parent is truly without income. The truly indigent noncustodial parent who learns that a support order has been entered by means of a default judgment should immediately contact the CSE agency to request a modification of the order. Failure to act causes the indigent noncustodial parent to accumulate debt that cannot be forgiven.

A noncustodial parent who becomes delinquent in paying child support pursuant to a court order becomes subject to all of the severe enforcement actions discussed in Chapter 6. The enforcement measures used by CSE agencies to collect delinquent support payments often make a bad situation worse. The parent might have 50 percent of his or her wages garnished, lose his or her driver's license, be unable to secure credit or loans, and incur greater debt from the interest that accumulates on child support arrearages. Any parent whose court order "reserves" child support is subject to a modification review without notice upon verification of employment.

Review requests by custodial parents

A child support order obtained 10 years earlier might have no relationship to the noncustodial parent's present ability to pay support, because the noncustodial parent's income could have increased substantially during that period. Even though the noncustodial parent may have the ability to pay a larger amount of support, he or she does not owe any support that exceeds the amount in the support order. A custodial parent must request a modification of an outdated support order if he or she believes that more child support is justified. Just as a support order cannot be retroactively modified to forgive arrearages that have accumulated, a support order cannot be retroactively modified to create arrearages based on a higher ability to pay.

The agency usually mails forms to the parent who requests a modification review. These forms require the parent to provide information on his or her income and expenses. The agency normally requires the requesting parent to submit copies of current pay stubs, tax returns, and verification of childcare expenses, if applicable. When the agency has received the completed income and expense information from the requesting parent, it will contact the other parent to obtain the same information.

A custodial parent currently receiving AFDC is not required to complete an income and expense form, though he or she may request a review for modification of the child support order. If the noncustodial parent has experienced a substantial increase in income, the modification of the support order might enable the custodial parent to stop receiving welfare.

The CSE agency normally allows up to 30 days for the parent who has requested a modification review to return the income and expense forms, and usually terminates the review if the parent who requested it fails to return the completed income and expense forms.

A parent who experiences difficulties in completing the income and expense forms or is unable to understand portions of the forms, and is unable to talk with someone at the CSE agency, should complete as much as possible and return the forms and pay stubs or other forms of income verification. If the caseworker wants additional information, he or she will contact the requesting parent. The sooner the forms are returned to the CSE agency, the sooner the agency can review the case for a modification.

The parent who has not requested the review does not normally benefit by failing to cooperate. The CSE agency usually can obtain that parent's gross income information from governmental databases. The income and expense declaration gives him or her an opportunity to inform the agency and the court of additional facts that can cause a reduction in that parent's income for determining a child support order.

If the nonrequesting parent does not cooperate with the agency, the agency either conducts a modification review without the non-requesting parent's information, or requests that the court issue a subpoena ordering the nonrequesting parent to appear with the requested information.

When the custodial parent has requested that a review be conducted for a possible upward modification of the support order, and has submitted income and expense declaration forms to the CSE agency, the agency notifies the noncustodial parent that a modification review will be conducted, and requests that the noncustodial parent also complete and return an income and expense declaration. Many noncustodial parents do not return their income and expense declarations to the agency. They believe that if they fail to return the forms or provide information, no review will take place. Unfortunately for these parents, all that is required is that both parents be given an opportunity to submit information. When the noncustodial parent does not respond, the review process proceeds without that parent's input.

The CSE agency usually allows the responding parent 30 days to send his or her financial information. Once the agency has obtained all of the documentation voluntarily submitted by both parents, and has gathered information on the parents' incomes from state and federal databases, the staff conducts a review of the case. The agency follows state-established support guidelines (discussed in Chapter 5) to determine if a modification increasing (upward modification) or decreasing (downward modification) the child support order is warranted.

If a modification of the support order is warranted, the nonrequesting parent can be given an opportunity to voluntarily stipulate to a modification of the support order. If the case involves a custodial parent receiving AFDC, that parent's agreement to a modification of the support order is not needed. In an AFDC case, the CSE agency makes the decision for the custodial parent on the appropriate amount of the order.

If the custodial parent is not receiving welfare (a nonaid case), a stipulated modification requires the agreement of both parents. If both parents in a nonaid case do not agree to stipulate to a modification, or if the noncustodial parent in an aid case does not stipulate to a modification, the agency files with the court an appropriate petition—a motion for modification, an order to show cause for modification, or some similar legal action—requesting that the court order a modification of the support order. The CSE agency must serve the modification petition or order to show cause upon the noncustodial parent.

Once the notice of motion or order to show cause has been served on the noncustodial parent, the court assigns a date that it will hear the case, and the noncustodial parent is notified of the date of the hearing. The CSE agency commonly sends the noncustodial parent a written calculation showing the requested modified child support amount, and subpoenas the nonaid custodial parent to appear in court on the date for hearing the petition. The agency does not ordinarily require the AFDC custodial parent to attend the modification hearing, but he or she is welcome to attend. At any time prior to the hearing date, the noncustodial parent may contact the agency to sign a stipulated modification of the court order. If a support order is modified by stipulation, a court appearance is usually not required.

Parents in a nonaid case are not required to follow the state's support guidelines. If parents begin to negotiate the level of a support order in a nonaid case, the CSE agency can function as an intermediary between them. Negotiated and mediated support orders can be established by the signatures of both parents, and this can be accomplished through the mail. The advantage to parents who are able to agree on a modification is that they can avoid the necessity of a court appearance and expedite the modification process.

The noncustodial parent in an AFDC case

The noncustodial parent in a case in which the custodial parent is receiving AFDC may request a review of the case for a possible downward modification. If a downward modification is justified, it is initiated by the signature of the noncustodial parent to a stipulated order. When the noncustodial parent signs the stipulated order modifying child support in an AFDC case, the agency files the stipulated order with the court, and when approved by the judge or administrative officer, the new amount becomes effective. No court appearance is necessary. In fact, this process can be handled by mail.

If the noncustodial parent has requested a modification review and disagrees with the decision of the CSE agency on that review, the noncustodial parent can file with the court a petition or request for an order to show cause to modify the support order. The agency then must respond to the petition and the court resolves the issue.

The noncustodial parent in a nonaid case

If a noncustodial parent in a nonaid case requests a review for a downward modification, the CSE agency must obtain financial information from the custodial parent to determine whether a modification is warranted. Should the custodial parent refuse to provide the information, the CSE agency requests the court to fix a date for a hearing on the requested modification, and usually issues a subpoena requiring the custodial parent to attend the hearing and to produce the requested information.

Every parent with a child support order is entitled to request that the agency handling the case review the court order for modification. When both parents cooperate with the agency, the process is simple and expeditious, but when the agency must petition the court to resolve a dispute over a modification, the process can take many months.

Chapter 8

Interstate Actions

For many years, interstate child support cases were regulated by the Uniform Reciprocal Enforcement of Support Act (URESA) and the Revised Uniform Reciprocal Enforcement of Support Act (RURESA). These statutes established the procedures and policies that governed the manner in which states worked to establish and enforce paternity and support orders when the noncustodial parent and the children lived in different states.

The interstate process was paper-intensive. If an interstate child-support case did not already have a paternity adjudication and a court order for support, the state in which the children lived (the "initiating state") had to prepare a full package to be sent to the other state. This package included paternity forms completed by the mother, and numerous other documents requested by the state in which the non-custodial parent resided (the "receiving state") to establish an order for the support of the children.

If the noncustodial parent was already subject to a court order for support of the children, the initiating state could send a shorter version of the interstate child support petition, called an interstate transmittal, which simply requested that the receiving state register and enforce the support order.

Some of the URESA processes could be slow-moving and time-consuming. Moreover, the receiving state was free to modify a court order for support made in the initiating state, so that the court order would conform to the receiving state's child support standards. Some times receiving states declined to collect support arrearages or reimbursement because of the receiving state's statute of limitations governing collection of arrearages.

Some cases in which the noncustodial parent had moved from state to state had multiple and conflicting orders obtained in different jurisdictions that created confusion in determining which order was to be enforced.

Frequent moves made it possible for noncustodial parents to avoid paying child support and produced a bureaucratic nightmare. Once a noncustodial parent was located, child support enforcement staff from many agencies had to engage in a comprehensive accounting process to determine the precise amount of child support owed by the noncustodial parent. Employers who had been served with conflicting wage assignments from different states did not know which wage assignment to honor. Enforcing these court orders was further complicated by conflicting state laws.

A further complication was caused when a custodial parent moved from state to state. The custodial parent's receipt of AFDC in more than one state caused numerous separate state civil actions for child support and reimbursement for welfare expenditures. These multiple civil actions for child support produced multiple billings sent to the noncustodial parent for different amounts covering the same periods of time.

The birth of UIFSA

In 1992, the havoc caused by this conflicting system of child support laws motivated employers, child support experts, and political leaders to reach agreement on a new interstate model law to simplify the processes governing interstate child support cases. This law, called the Uniform Interstate Family Support Act (UIFSA), was first adopted by the National Conference of Commissioners on Uniform State Laws in 1992 and was modified in 1996. As of June 1, 1996, 33 states and the District of Columbia had fully implemented UIFSA. Some of the remaining 17 states modified their URESA statutes to conform to some of the requirements mandated by UIFSA. The Welfare Reform Act requires all states to fully implement UIFSA by January 1, 1998.

UIFSA allows states to exercise jurisdiction over a noncustodial parent who resides in another state in establishing paternity and enforcing and establishing child support orders. UIFSA requires states to enforce against their own residents the orders made by other states, without requiring that out-of-state orders be registered in the state where the noncustodial parent lives. UIFSA also regulates the power of the state in which the noncustodial parent lives to modify an out-of-state support order. Finally, UIFSA makes employers subject to the jurisdiction of child support orders entered in other states, even if the employers do not do business in the states that enter the support orders.

The most significant change produced by UIFSA is the elimination of multiple-state child support orders. Under UIFSA there will be only one court order for the support of a child, no matter how often the custodial parent and child or the noncustodial parent moves. Once a child support order has been entered by a state, that state will have exclusive and continuing jurisdiction over the case as long as that state remains the residence of the noncustodial parent, the custodial parent, or the child for whose benefit the support order is issued. Other states must give full faith and credit to the support order of the initiating state.

Streamlining the process of interstate support enforcement will produce significant time savings for CSE agencies. New forms are being developed to make the UIFSA process easier to implement. Many states have begun to use administrative process instead of the judicial process to handle child support-related legal actions. The Welfare Reform Act advocates administrative process for child support actions, and the language in UIFSA has been changed to call the judicial bodies handling child support orders tribunals, instead of referring to these bodies as courts. An administrative process produces administrative orders instead of court orders, and the obtaining of administrative orders is expected to be quicker and easier. Many states are already changing from the judicial process to the administrative process to handle *all* child support actions—not just URESA/UIFSA cases. These changes will be implemented on an ongoing basis over the next few years.

UIFSA has simplified the procedures governing the rules of evidence and the rules regulating discovery for hearings in child support cases. Witnesses are allowed to testify by telephone. Legal documents transmitted by fax machines may be introduced as evidence, and process may be served by the U.S. Postal Service, fax, or other means in place of personal service by a sheriff or process server.

Parents can employ private attorneys to represent them during UIFSA proceedings, or they can request the services of the CSE agency. Each state's Attorney General's office is responsible for ensuring that the CSE agency in their state properly performs its duties under UIFSA. CSE agencies must keep the interested parties—CSE agencies, custodial parent, noncustodial parent, and attorneys of the parents—informed of all important developments in a case. Parents may also file their own UIFSA action in another state, with or without benefit of private counsel or the CSE agency. Parents can also request adjudication of paternity only in an interstate action, while not requesting that a child support order be obtained at the same time.

UIFSA declares that the laws of all states enacted under URESA be recognized and enforced, and that the laws of all states shall be used to enforce interstate support actions.

"Long arm" statutes

UIFSA attempts to resolve the question of how a state can obtain personal jurisdiction over a noncustodial parent who lives in another jurisdiction by expanding the use of "long arm" statutes. If a state agency handling a child support case in the initiating jurisdiction (the state where the custodial parent and children live) does not want to send a full UIFSA petition to the responding state (the state in which the noncustodial parent lives), the initiating state can still effect service of process on the noncustodial parent in the other state. The initiating state's use of "long arm" jurisdiction eliminates the need for the state of residence of the noncustodial parent to become involved in the child support action and speeds the establishment of personal jurisdiction over the noncustodial parent.

UIFSA recognizes several different situations in which an initiating state can exercise "long arm" jurisdiction. An initiating state can gain jurisdiction over a nonresident noncustodial parent when the child lived in the initiating state with the noncustodial parent; when the noncustodial parent lived in the initiating state and provided prenatal expenses or support for the child; when the child was conceived in the initiating state as a result of sexual intercourse between the noncustodial parent and the custodial parent; and when the noncustodial parent submits to the jurisdiction of the initiating state by consent or by filing an Answer to a child support petition.

If a noncustodial parent contests the jurisdiction of the initiating state, the initiating state may then file a UIFSA petition in the state where the noncustodial parent resides. A noncustodial parent who contests the jurisdiction of another state must usually hire an attorney to represent him or her. Jurisdictional fights usually produce lengthy hearings, and although they may delay the child support action, they usually do not stop it. If a court or administrative officer determines that the initiating state has jurisdiction over the nonresident noncustodial parent, the court or administrative officer can hold the noncustodial parent liable to pay sanctions, the attorney fees of the custodial parent, and other related costs and expenses resulting from the proceedings.

Registration of foreign support orders

A CSE agency in the initiating state may request the jurisdiction in which the noncustodial parent lives to register and enforce an existing child support order. If the agency is unable to utilize a "long arm" statute to gain jurisdiction over the noncustodial parent, or the employer of the noncustodial parent in another state refuses to honor a wage assignment issued by an out-of-state court, the initiating state may send a URESA or UIFSA petition to the responding state.

The easiest method of enforcing an existing out-of-state order is registration of the order. Registration once produced confusion over which state's laws apply to an out-of-state order registered in another state. Many receiving states have applied their own laws to enforce a registered support order, even when they have conflicted with the laws that produced the registered order in the initiating jurisdiction.

Registration of an out-of-state support order is a necessary prerequisite for a state to enforce a support order issued outside of its jurisdiction. To register an out-of-state support order the responding state files with its own courts a form commonly entitled "Registration of Foreign Support Order." The word foreign means simply that the order came from outside the jurisdiction of the state receiving it; the order can be from a different county, state, or country. The CSE agency then serves the Registration of Foreign Support Order on the noncustodial parent and advises him or her that the registering jurisdiction has assumed the responsibility to enforce the order.

Under the laws in effect prior to UIFSA, the CSE agency could not take any action to enforce the out-of-state support order prior to its registration. Thus, the agency in the responding state could not serve a wage assignment on the noncustodial parent's employer, and could not modify the out-of-state order until it had been registered in the responding state. The noncustodial parent was generally given 20 days in which to dispute the registration before the agency could take legal action to enforce the order. Even after the 20-day waiting period had expired, some employers refused to honor wage assignments issued on a registered child support order.

UIFSA has significantly affected the process of registering out-of-state support orders. The most important change is that employers who receive an income-withholding order (wage assignment) issued by a court in another state must honor it without the benefit of having the court order and wage assignment registered in the state in which the employer's business is located. This "long arm" process of serving wage assignments should reduce the number of UIFSA petitions and simplify the process of enforcing a support order, because the "long arm" service of wage assignments will essentially eliminate the need to register support orders

As of the writing of this book, only employers located in states that have enacted UIFSA are honoring "long arm" service of wage assignments. Some employers in states that have not yet adopted UIFSA continue to require the initiating state to begin an interstate action by registering the court order in the employer's state, before honoring a wage assignment. The adoption of UIFSA by all states will produce a uniform practice of "long arm" service of wage assignments on employers, as is intended by UIFSA.

A noncustodial parent may contest the validity or enforcement of a registered support order only if the order is allegedly invalid, superseded, or no longer in effect. The process of registering a support order does not set or change the child support obligation—registration only moves legal jurisdiction of the case from one state or county to another. The noncustodial parent who claims that the underlying support order is invalid, has been superseded, or is no longer in effect can defend an allegation of noncompliance with the registered order or can contest the method of enforcement on alleged arrearages by petitioning the court to vacate the registration. If the noncustodial parent fails to properly contest the validity or enforcement of the order, the registration of the out-of-state support order is confirmed.

If the noncustodial parent requests a hearing to contest the registration of the out-of-state support order, a hearing is set and all parties are given notice of the date, time, and place of the hearing. A noncustodial parent who contests the validity or enforcement of a registered court order, or who seeks to vacate the order, has the burden to prove that the initiating state lacked personal jurisdiction over that parent when the order was issued; that the order was obtained fraudulently; that the order has been vacated or paid in full; or that the statute of limitations precludes enforcement of the order.

When the initiating and responding states have conflicting statutes of limitations on enforcing child support orders, the state with the longer statute of limitations controls. If the noncustodial parent can prove one of these defenses to registering a support order, the noncustodial parent can request that enforcement of the registered order be "stayed" until the lawfulness of the support order has been established.

UIFSA has also simplified the process of registering a support order. Under UIFSA enforcement of the registered order may begin immediately; the CSE agency does not have to wait until the expiration of the 20-day period for the noncustodial parent to challenge the registration in order to take enforcement action on the registered order. Finally, and *very important* to remember, the receiving state is only empowered to enforce the registered court order; the receiving state may not modify that order. The registered court order retains the terms ordered by the court in the initiating state.

Employer obligations under UIFSA

Under UIFSA, wage assignments no longer must be certified and served upon an employer in order to be valid. Either the custodial parent (if he or she does not have an open case with a CSE agency) or a representative from the CSE agency may send a copy of the wage assignment to the employer by first-class mail. The employer must provide a copy of the wage assignment to the noncustodial parent and treat the order issued in another state as if it had been issued by a court or tribunal of the employer's state. The employer is required to honor the terms of the wage assignment and distribute the funds according to the instructions on the wage assignment. All wage assignments must be sum-certain, stating the amount of and the time frame for the deductions. Health insurance orders issued by a court in the initiating state must also be honored according to the terms of the orders.

Employers must follow the laws of the state of the noncustodial parent's primary place of employment in establishing employer's fees for processing a wage assignment, in determining the maximum deductions permitted, in fixing the time frames for implementing the order, and in forwarding the payments to the custodial parent. An employer that fails to comply with a wage assignment issued by a court in another state can be penalized for this failure according to the laws of the state in which the employer is located.

The same rules discussed above apply when employers receive multiple wage assignments on the same parent. Employers who comply with a wage assignment from another state are not subject to civil liability resulting from the employer's implementation of the wage assignment.

These new rules will help reduce confusion over multiple wage assignments from other states, allowing employers to easily accept and implement these wage assignments without fear of adverse consequences for their compliance.

Under UIFSA a noncustodial parent may contest the validity or enforcement of a wage assignment received from another state. When contesting an out-of-state wage assignment the noncustodial parent must give notice of the dispute to the person or the agency that served the wage assignment on the employer, and to all employers involved. However, the only viable claims that will defeat the service of a wage assignment are: 1) an error in the amount of current support owed, 2) death of the child for whose benefit the wage assignment was served, or 3) the person on whose employer the wage assignment was served is not the obligor named in the underlying child support order. A noncustodial parent may not contest the amount of current child support set in the support order in order to contest a wage assignment.

Long arm enforcement of a support order by service of a wage assignment does not work well when the noncustodial parent is self-employed or has hidden his or her assets. If the noncustodial parent is not reachable by a wage assignment, the initiating state must send a UIFSA petition to the responding state, which must register the order and begin enforcement actions against assets that are not reachable by wage assignment.

Controlling court orders

One of the goals of UIFSA is the elimination of multiple court orders on the same case from different states. Thousands of child support cases have multiple court orders for support. In the meantime, UIFSA provides that one of the multiple court orders for support must be declared to be the controlling order. The court order chosen will be the one issued by the state that has continuing, exclusive jurisdiction over the child support case. The first criterion will be the state of the child's residence. When conflicting support orders have been issued by different courts within the same state, the most recent order will be considered the controlling order.

If a court or administrative hearing officer needs to decide which is the controlling support order, he or she must gather and review all of the conflicting orders. He or she must inform all of the competing jurisdictions of the decision on which order is selected as the controlling order.

A responding state must enforce the controlling support order according to the laws of the state that issued it. This requirement will have a dramatic effect in preventing noncustodial parents from moving to avoid enforcement of a child support order, as some noncustodial parents have purposefully moved to states in which the laws affecting enforcement of a child support order were less stringent. For example, California has no statute of limitations on judgments; a judgment can be enforced indefinitely. New York, however, does not generally enforce judgments to collect arrearages older than seven years.

Registration for modification of child support orders

Prior to UIFSA, a receiving state that registered the sending state's court order could issue a new order or modify the other state's order. This practice resulted in the duplication of thousands of support orders. UIFSA prohibits a receiving state from modifying another state's child support or paternity order, unless the receiving state has controlling, exclusive jurisdiction over it, thus ensuring that the receiving state gives full faith and credit to the original order.

The following four cases should assist in explaining how the newly enacted UIFSA policies regarding modification of out-of-state court orders will work in a practical setting.

Case #1: The custodial parent resides with the child in California. California issued a child support order and maintains continuing, exclusive jurisdiction over the order. The noncustodial parent lives in Montana. It does not matter which parent requests a modification; a California court is the only court with authority to modify the California order.

Case #2: The same custodial parent and child as in Case #1 have moved to Texas. The noncustodial parent still lives in Montana. The California support order follows the custodial parent and child to Texas. However, since none of the parties lives in California, California no longer has continuing exclusive jurisdiction over the support order. The state that has authority to conduct the modification is Montana or Texas, depending on which parent requests it.

The reason for this procedure is simple: to prevent either parent from seeking a "hometown advantage" by moving to a state perceived to be favorable to that parent and then seeking a modification in the new "home state." This procedure also prevents the noncustodial parent from purposely moving to a state with a lower cost of living (hence a lower child support schedule) than the state that issued the order. Likewise, a custodial parent may not seek an upward modification of a support order based on a move to a state that has higher child support guidelines based on a higher cost of living.

Case #3: The custodial parent, the child, and the noncustodial parent live in Texas. The original support order was issued by a California court, and this original order has not yet been modified. Because all of the parties have moved from California, California has lost continuing exclusive jurisdiction over the case and its support order. In this situation, both parents must agree in writing that the state of Texas has authority to register the California support order and modify it, since all parties reside in Texas. If one of the parties refuses to agree, the matter is referred to a judge or administrative officer for resolution.

Case #4: After the Texas court in Case #3 modifies the original California support order, the custodial parent and child move back to California. The Texas-modified support order is controlling and California must recognize the Texas-modified support order. California may not change the modified Texas support order without the consent of the noncustodial parent in Texas. California could, however, resume its enforcement of the modified Texas order on principles of law that are not subject to modification. For example, California can enforce and collect support arrearages without regard to a statute of limitations, since California does not have a statute of limitations on collection of child support.

Certain components of a child support order are not subject to modification. One such component is the age of emancipation. If a California marriage dissolution judgment ordered child support to be paid until the child turned 21, Texas may not modify the support order, even though the age of emancipation in Texas might be age 18. However, when a support order is registered without modification, the age of emancipation that controls that order is the age established by the state that has continuing exclusive jurisdiction of the case. That law supersedes the law of emancipation of the receiving state. If California's age of emancipation is age 18 and Texas' age of emancipation is age 21, when California registers and enforces a Texas support order, California must enforce the order until the child reaches the age of 21 years.

In addition to interstate registrations of support orders, some orders must be registered in different counties within the same state. When a custodial parent moves to a different county within the same state, the new county of residence of the custodial parent must register a support order issued in another county of the state. While the courts of one county do not face personal jurisdictional problems in intercounty registrations, the new county of residence of the custodial parent must assume jurisdiction over the support order. Jurisdiction to enforce the order is determined by the county in which the child resides. The new registration process is used, the noncustodial parent is notified that the county of the child's residence is now enforcing the court order, and the former county of the child's residence transfers its case to the new county.

International support enforcement

There are numerous foreign countries with which each state in the United States has reciprocal child support enforcement agreements. The Welfare Reform Act, UIFSA, and URESA all contain provisions to specify how we are to work with other countries on child support enforcement.

Any foreign country that has formal procedures for the establishment and enforcement of child support obligations owed to residents of the United States is declared a reciprocating country. Likewise, any participating foreign country that wishes to pursue enforcement of its child support orders against residents of the United States may do so.

When a state enters into a mutual agreement for child support enforcement with another country, the components of the agreement must be acceptable to both jurisdictions. Reciprocity can be revoked if it is determined that the foreign country's procedures are unsatisfactory.

In order for any state in the United States to agree to enter into a reciprocal agreement with a foreign country, the foreign country's child support procedures and standards must be acceptable to the United States. This includes standards for the establishment of paternity and child support orders, enforcement of child support orders, the collection and distribution of support moneys, and agreement that all legal and administrative procedures will be provided at no cost to residents of the United States.

The foreign country must also designate a specific agency with the authority to facilitate child support enforcement for both the United States and the other country. The other country must guarantee that it will ensure compliance with these standards.

In reciprocal agreements, the United States agrees to be responsible to facilitate child support enforcement by developing uniform procedures and forms. Foreign countries can request the Federal Parent Locator Service (FPLS) to identify the state of residence of any noncustodial parent who resides in the United States.

International child support cases are initiated by URESA or UIFSA petitions. If the custodial parent resides in the United States and the noncustodial parent resides in a participating foreign country, the CSE agency can file a UIFSA petition in that country. The foreign country then initiates the required legal actions against the noncustodial parent; obtains an order for paternity, child support, and medical support; and then enforces the support order. In cases that have an existing United States court order, the foreign country enforces the United States' order against the noncustodial parent.

If the custodial parent and child reside in a foreign country and the noncustodial parent resides in the United States, the country in which the custodial parent resides can file a petition in the state where the noncustodial parent lives and can request that a CSE agency in that state establish a child support order or enforce an existing order issued in the foreign country.

Although differences in laws and procedures sometimes cause complications, child support enforcement can be done successfully on an international basis. For a sample list of the participating countries with which California has reciprocity, refer to Chapter 9. If a noncustodial parent resides in one of these countries, the custodial parent in California can pursue a case by filing an application with the custodial parent's local CSE agency. Although many states probably have reciprocal agreements with most of the countries that have agreements with California, each state enters into its own reciprocal child support enforcement agreements with foreign countries. Parents should contact the CSE agency in their area to determine which foreign countries have reciprocal child support agreements with their home state.

Because URESA, RURESA, UIFSA, and international support enforcement laws are complicated, we advise parents involved in such actions to contact the CSE agency in their area for clarification on the laws and procedures in effect in the state in which they live. In most instances, CSE agencies handle URESA/UIFSA issues on behalf of custodial parents, although agencies also respond to requests submitted by noncustodial parents.

UIFSA/URESA is a specialized field of family law practice. Noncustodial parents who find themselves on the receiving end of a UIFSA or URESA action that involves a foreign country and who want to contest the action should consult an attorney who has experience in UIFSA/URESA. General practice family law attorneys may not be aware of the underlying laws and procedures governing UIFSA/URESA and foreign countries. Likewise, CSE agencies usually assign the UIFSA/URESA cases involving foreign countries to an attorney within the agency who is knowledgeable about UIFSA/URESA and foreign reciprocal agreements.

Chapter 9

United States Listing of Central Registries

Every state has a Central Registry that contains the IV-D agency and State Parent Locator Service (SPLS). Parents wishing to find out the location of the CSE or other government agency in their area can contact the Central Registry in the state where they reside. The Central Registry will provide you with the name, address, and phone number of the CSE agency, Department of Social Services, County Recorder, County Clerk, County Assessor, Parental Kidnapping Case Assistance, and County Sheriff's office in your area.

Alabama
Child Support Enforcement Division
Department of Human Resources
50 Ripley St.
Montgomery, AL 36130
334-242-9300
Fax: 334-242-0606

Alaska
Child Support Enforcement Agency
Department of Revenue—MS 10
550 W. 7th Ave., Ste. 310
Anchorage, AK 99501-6699
907-269-6910
Fax: 907-269-6650

Arizona
Division of Child Support
  Enforcement
Department of Economic Security
P.O. Box 40458—Site Code 966 C
Phoenix, AZ 85067
602-252-4045
Fax: 602-248-3126

Arkansas
Department of Finance and
  Administration
Office of Child Support Enforcement
P.O. Box 8133
Little Rock, AR 72203
501-682-8406
Fax: 501-682-6002

California
Department of Justice
P.O. Box 903199 (mailing address)
1300 I St., 11th Fl. (office address)
Sacramento, CA 94203-3199
916-323-5650
Fax: 916-323-5669

Colorado
Child Support Enforcement Section
Department of Human Services
1575 Sherman St., 2nd Fl.
Denver, CO 80203-1714
303-866-5965
Fax: 303-866-2214

Connecticut
Support Enforcement Administration
287 Main St., 3rd Fl.
East Hartford, CT 06118-1885
860-569-6274
Fax: 860-569-6557

Delaware
Division of Child Support Enforcement
Department of Health and
 Social Services
P.O. Box 904
New Castle, DE 19720
302-369-2135, ext. 218
Fax: 302-369-2171

District of Columbia
Office of Paternity and Child
 Support Enforcement
Department of Human Services
800 9th St. SW, 2nd Fl.
Washington, DC 20024-2485
202-645-5368
Fax: 202-645-4102

Florida
Child Support Enforcement
Department of Revenue
P.O. Box 8030
Tallahassee, FL 32314-8030
904-922-9555
Fax: 904-414-1698

Georgia
Department of Human Resources
Office of Child Support Recovery
P.O. Box 38070
Atlanta, GA 30334-0070
404-657-3875
Fax: 404-657-1462

Hawaii
Child Support Enforcement
P.O. Box 1860
Honolulu, HI 96805-1860
808-587-3754
Fax: 808-587-3717

Idaho
Idaho Bureau of Child Support
 Services
P.O. Box 83720
Boise, ID 83720-0036
208-334-5710
Fax: 208-334-0666

Illinois
Department of Public Aid
Division of Child Support
 Enforcement
P.O. Box 19405 (mailing address)
201 S. Grand St. East (office address)
Springfield, IL 62794-9405
217-782-0420
Fax: 217-524-6049

Indiana
Child Support Bureau
Family and Social Services
 Administration
402 W. Washington St., Rm. W360
Indianapolis, IN 46204
317-232-3447
Fax: 317-233-4925

Iowa
Bureau of Collections
Department of Human Services
P.O. Box 9218
Des Moines, IA 50306
515-242-6099
Fax: 515-281-6632

Kansas
Child Support Enforcement Program
P.O. Box 497 (mailing address)
300 SW Oakley St.
Biddle Building, 1st Fl. (office address)
Topeka, KS 66601-0497
913-296-3237
Fax: 913-296-5206

Kentucky
Division of Child Support
   Enforcement
Department for Social Insurance
275 E. Main St., 6th Fl.
Frankfort, KY 40621
502-564-2285, ext. 435
Fax: 502-564-5988

Louisiana
Support Enforcement Services
P.O. Box 94065
Baton Rouge, LA 70804-4065
504-342-4781
Fax: 504-342-7397

Maine
Department of Human Services
Division of Support Enforcement
State House, Station 11
Augusta, ME 04333
207-287-2886
Fax: 207-287-5096

Maryland
Child Support Enforcement
   Administration
311 West Saratoga St., Rm. 311
Baltimore, MD 21201
410-767-7052
Fax: 410-333-8992

Massachusetts
Department of Revenue
Child Support Enforcement Division
P.O. Box 4068
Wakefield, MA 01880-3095
617-213-1000
Fax: 617-246-3856

Michigan
Office of Child Support
Family Independence Agency
P.O. Box 30478
Lansing, MI 48909-7978
517-335-0892
Fax: 517-373-4980

Minnesota
Office of Child Support Enforcement
444 Lafayette Rd., 4th Fl.
St. Paul, MN 55155-3846
612-296-2696
Fax: 612-297-4450

Mississippi
Division of Child Support
   Enforcement
Department of Human Services
P.O. Box 352
Jackson, MS 39205
601-359-4869
Fax: 601-359-4415

Missouri
Division of Child Support
   Enforcement
P.O. Box 1468 (mailing address)
2701 W. Main St. (office address)
Jefferson City, MO 65102-1527
573-751-4224
Fax: 314-751-1257

Montana
Child Support Enforcement Division
Department of Public Health &
 Human Services
P.O. Box 202943 (mailing address)
3975 North Montana, Ste. 112
Helena, MT 59620-2943
406-442-7278
Fax: 406-444-1370

Nebraska
Child Support Enforcement Office
Department of Social Services
P.O. Box 95026 (mailing address)
301 Centennial Mall So.,
 5th Fl. (office address)
Lincoln, NE 68509-5026
402-471-9160
Fax: 402-471-9455

Nevada
Child Support Enforcement Program
Nevada State Welfare Division
2527 N. Carson St.
Carson City, NV 89710
702-687-4713
Fax: 702-684-8026

New Hampshire
Office of Child Support
Office of Program Support
6 Hazen Dr.
Concord, NH 03301
603-271-4428
Fax: 603-271-4771

New Jersey
Administrative Office of the Courts
Child Support Enforcement Services
CN-960
Trenton, NJ 08625
609-292-1087
Fax: 609-984-3630

New Mexico
Child Support Enforcement Bureau
Human Services Department
P.O. Box 25109
Santa Fe, NM 87504
505-827-1982
Fax: 505-827-7285

New York
Office of Child Support Enforcement
1 Commerce Plaza
P.O. Box 125
Albany, NY 12260-0125
518-474-9092
Fax: 518-486-3127

North Carolina
Child Support Enforcement
Department of Human Resources
Division of Social Services
100 E. Six Forks Rd.
Raleigh, NC 27609-7724
919-571-4114
Fax: 919-881-2280

North Dakota
Child Support Enforcement Agency
Department of Human Services
P.O. Box 7190
1929 N. Washington St.
Bismarck, ND 58507-7190
701-328-5491
Fax: 701-328-5497

Ohio
Child Support Enforcement
Bureau of Direct Services
Department of Human Services
30 E. Board St., 31st Fl.
Columbus, OH 43266-0423
614-752-6567
Fax: 614-466-6613

Oklahoma
Child Support Enforcement Unit
P.O. Box 53552
Oklahoma City, OK 73152
405-522-2765
Fax: 405-522-4570

Oregon
Department of Justice
Support Enforcement Division
1495 Edgewater NW, Ste. 290
Salem, OR 97304
503-373-7300
Fax: 503-373-7340

Pennsylvania
Bureau of Child Support Enforcement
P.O. Box 8018
Harrisburg, PA 17105
717-783-9684
Fax: 717-787-9706

Rhode Island
Child Support Services
77 Dorrance St.
Providence, RI 02903
401-277-2847
Fax: 401-277-6674

South Carolina
Child Support Enforcement Division
P.O. Box 1469
Columbia, SC 29020-1469
803-737-5875
Fax: 803-737-6032

South Dakota
Office of Child Support Enforcement
700 Governors Dr.
Pierre, SD 57501-2291
605-773-3641
Fax: 605-773-6834

Tennessee
Office of Child Support Services
Department of Human Services
Citizens Plaza Bldg., 12th Fl.
400 Deaderick St.
Nashville, TN 37248-7400
615-313-4880
Fax: 615-532-2791

Texas
Office of the Attorney General
P.O. Box 12017
Austin, TX 78711-2017
512-463-2181
Fax: 512-834-9695

Utah
Office of Recovery Services
Bureau of Child Support Services
P.O. Box 45011 (mailing address)
100 S. 515 East (office address)
Salt Lake City, UT 84145-0011
801-536-8642
Fax: 801-536-8833

Vermont
Office of Child Support
103 South Main St.
Waterbury, VT 05676
802-241-2306
Fax: 802-244-1483

Virginia
Virginia Department of Social
  Services
730 E. Broad St., 4th Fl.
Richmond, VA 23219-1849
804-692-1491
Fax: 804-692-1405

Washington State
Office of Support Enforcement
P.O. Box 9008 (mailing address)
724 Quince St. SE (office address)
Olympia, WA 98507-9008
360-586-2125
Fax: 360-586-3094

West Virginia
Child Support Enforcement Division
Department of Health and Human
    Resources, State Capitol Complex
Building 6, Rm. 817
Charleston, WV 25305
304-558-3608
Fax: 304-558-1121

Wisconsin
Bureau of Child Support
Division of Economic Support
P.O. Box 7935, Rm. 382
Madison, WI 53707-7935
608-267-0924
Fax 608-266-4828

Wyoming
Child Support Enforcement Section
Department of Family Services
Hathaway Building, 3rd Fl.
Cheyenne, WY 82002-0490
307-777-7603
Fax: 307-777-3693

American Samoa
Office of the Attorney General
P.O. Box 7
Utulei, American Samoa 96799
9-011-684-633-4163
Fax: 9-011-684-633-1838

Guam
Office of the Attorney General—
    Family Division
Pacific News Building, Ste. 701
238 Archbishop F.C. Flores St.
Agana, Guam 96910
671-475-3660, 3663
Fax: 671-477-6118

Northern Mariana Islands
Commonwealth of the Northern
    Mariana Islands
Office of the Attorney General
Civil Division—Capitol Hill
Administration Building, 2nd Fl.
Saipan, MP 96950
9-011-670-664-2331
Fax: 9-011-670-664-2349

Puerto Rico
Department of the Family
Administration for Child Support
    Enforcement
P.O. Box 9023349
San Juan, PR 00902-3349
787-767-1894; 767-1500, ext. 2703
Fax: 787-282-7411

Virgin Islands
Division of Paternity and Child
    Support, Department of Justice
48B-50C Kronprindsens Gade
GRS Complex, 2nd Fl.
St. Thomas, VI 00802
809-774-5666
Fax: 809-775-3808

Federal Office of Child Support
    Enforcement (OCSE)
Department of Health/Human Services
370 L'Enfant Promenade SW
Washington, DC 20447
202-401-9200
Fax: 202-401-4683

The listing of the Central Registries located in the United States and its districts should serve you as a central resource. It provides you with a way to contact a governmental agency to which you can address questions and from which you can obtain additional information on the CSE system and its network. Parents can also call the Central Registry to obtain addresses and telephone numbers for other state and federal departments involved in the child support system, such as the Attorney General's office, FPLS, Department of Social Services, etc. Any Central Registry can refer you to another source if the information you request is not available through that registry's office.

Although some small states' offices are staffed with only one or two persons, the Central Registries are a state's central receiving point that directs all incoming UIFSA/URESA petitions to the appropriate child support agency in that state. Central Registries are also responsible for ensuring that the receiving CSE agency responds to the initiating CSE agency's request for action. Complaints regarding inaction by any jurisdiction on a child support case can also be reported to that state's Central Registry.

In addition to the states' Cental Registries, we've also provided a listing of countries with which California has reciprocity (pages 149-152). The countries with which a state has reciprocity vary from state to state. Contact your state's Central Registry to get its participating country list.

Sample international reciprocity directory

To handle cases in which the noncustodial parent resides outside the boundaries of the United States, each state has reciprocal agreements with many other countries. Custodial parents living in one of these countries can open a case in that country also, which can pursue the noncustodial parent in the United States.

That country and the state work together to establish and enforce paternity, child support, and medical support. The procedure followed is similar to the URESA/UIFSA procedures in effect for child support cases between states in the United States.

Parents who know that the noncustodial parent lives in any of these participating countries can contact the Central Registry or their local CSE agency and open a case. The agency will formally contact the country in which the noncustodial parent resides and child support enforcement actions will begin. The following is a complete listing of all countries with which the state of California has reciprocity. Contact your state for clarification on its participating country list.

Australia
International Civil Procedures Section
Attorney General's Department—
   Civil Law Division
50 Blackall St.
Barton ACT 2600
Australia
(011) 616-250-6723
Fax: (011) 616-250-5939

Austria
Bundesministerium fur Justiz
1070 Wien, Museumstrasse 7
   (office address)
1016 Wien, Postfach 63
   (mailing address)
Austria
(011) 431-521-522-134
Fax: (011) 431-521-522-727

Bermuda
Office of Family & Child Support
Magistrates' Court Building
23 Parliament St.
Hamilton HM 12
Bermuda
441-297-7923
Fax: 441-295-3321

Canada
Alberta
Alberta Justice
Maintenance Enforcement
P.O. Box 2404
Edmonton, Alberta
Canada T5J 3Z7
403-422-5554
Fax: 403-422-1215

British Columbia
Family Justice Programs
   Division
Reciprocals Program
8th Fl., 1001 Douglas St.
Victoria, British Columbia
Canada V8V 1X4
250-356-1555
Fax: 250-356-8902

Manitoba
Maintenance Enforcement Program
Department of Justice
2nd Fl., 405 Broadway
Winnipeg, Manitoba
Canada R3C 3L6
204-945-7133
Fax: 204-945-5449

New Brunswick
Registrar's Office
Court of Queen's Bench
Justice Building, Rm. 201
P.O. Box 6000
Fredericton, New Brunswick
Canada E3B 5HI
506-453-2452
Fax: 506-453-7921

Newfoundland/Labrador
Director of Support Enforcement
P.O. Box 2006
Corner Brook, Newfoundland
Canada A2H 6J8
709-637-2608
Fax: 709-634-9518

Northwest Territories
Commissioner
Government of the N.W.T.
P.O. Box 1320
Yellowknife, N.W.T.
Canada X1A 2L9
403-873-7400
Fax: 403-873-0223

Nova Scotia
Department of Justice
Maintenance Enforcement Program
Central Enrollment Unit
P.O. Box 803
Halifax, Nova Scotia
Canada B3J 2V2
902-424-8032
Fax: 902-424-2153

Ontario
Ministry of the Attorney General
Reciprocity Office
P.O. Box 640
Downsview, Ontario
Canada M3M 3A3
416-240-2410
Fax: 416-240-2405

Prince Edward Island
Maintenance Enforcement Office
42 Water St.
P.O. Box 2290
Charlottetown, P.E.I.
Canada C1A 8C1
902-368-6010
Fax: 902-368-0266

Quebec
Gouvernement du Quebec
Direction generales des affaires
   juridiques et legislatives
1200, route de l'Eglise, 2 etage
Canada G1V 4M1
418-644-7152
Fax: 418-646-1696

Saskatchewan
Maintenance Enforcement
Department of Justice
Box 2077
Regina, Saskatchewan
Canada S4P 4E8
306-787-8961
Fax: 306-787-1420

Yukon Territory
Maintenance Enforcement
   Program
Box 4066
Whitehorse, Yukon Territory
Canada Y1A 3S9
403-667-3038
Fax: 403-393-6212

Czech Republic
Ustredi Pro Mezinarodne Pravni
Ochranu Mladeze
Benesova 22
602 00 Brno
Czech Republic
(011) 425-4242-1286 Line 208
Fax: (011) 425-4221-2836

Fiji
Attorney General & Minister for Justice
Attorney General's Chambers
P.O. Box 2213
Government Buildings
Suva, Fiji
(011) 679-211-580
Fax: (011) 679-305-421

Finland
Ministry for Foreign Affairs
P.O. Box 176
SF-00161 Helsinki
Finland
Fax: (011) 358-013-415-755

France
Ministere de la justice
Bureau du droit international
et de l'entraide judiciaire
   internationale
en matiere civile et commerciale (L1)
13, Place Vendome
75042 Paris Cedex 01
(011) 331-4486-1475
Fax: (011) 331-4486-1406

Germany
Der Generalbundesanwalt
   beim Bundesgerichtshof
Zentrale Behorde
Neuenburger Strasse 15
10969 Berlin, Germany
(011) 4930-2538-8344
Fax: (011) 4930-2538-8397

Hungary
Igazsagugyi Miniszterium
Nemzetkozi Jogi Ugyosztaly
H-1055 Budapest
Szalay U, 16
Hungary
(011) 361-269-2020
Fax: (011) 361-269-2090

Ireland
Mr. Michael Gleeson
Department of Equality & Law
   Reform
43-49 Mespil Rd.
Dublin 4, Ireland
Fax: (011) 3531-667-0367

Mexico
Secretaria de Relaciones Exteriores
Consultoria Juridica
Homero #213, Piso 17
Col. Chapultepec Morales
Mexico, D.F., C.P. 11560
(011) 525-327-3218
Fax: (011) 525-327-3201

New Zealand
Department of Justice
Secretary for Justice
Private Bag 180
Wellington, New Zealand
(011) 644-4725-980
Fax: (011) 644-4723-362

Norway
Folketrygdkontoret for
   Utenlandssaker
Seksjon Familie
Postboks 8138 Dep.
N-0033 Oslo, Norway
(011) 4722-927-600
Fax: (011) 4722-481-230

Poland
Ministerstwo Sprawieldiwosci
Al. Ujazdowskie 11
00-950 Warsaw
Poland
(011) 482-628-4431
Fax: (011) 482-628-1692

Republic of South Africa
United States Embassy
Thibault House
225 Pretorius St.
Pretoria
Republic of South Africa

Slovak Republic
Centrum pre medzinarodno
Pravnu ochranu deti
   a mladeze
Spitalska 4-6
P.O. Box 57
814.99 Bratislava
Slovak Republic
(011) 427-362-895
Fax: (011) 427-362-895

Sweden
Forsakingskassan
Utlandskontoret
S-105 11
Stockholm, Sweden
(011) 468-676-1000
Fax: (011) 468-820-1966

United Kingdom
England and Wales
Lord Chancellor's Department
Selborne House, REMO Section
54/60 Victoria St.
London
SW1E 6QB
(011) 44-171-210-8645
Fax: (011) 44-171-210-8557

Northern Ireland
Northern Ireland Court Service
Courts Business Branch
Windsor House
Bedford St.
Belfast BT2 7LT
Northern Ireland
(011) 44-1232-328-594
Fax: (011) 44-1232-439-110

Scotland
Scottish Courts Administration
Hayweight House
23 Laruiston St.
Edinburgh EH3 9DQ
Scotland
(011) 44-131-299-9200
Fax: (011) 44-131-221-6894

Chapter 10

Age of Emancipation— Your Child Is Now an Adult

Used in child support cases, the term *emancipation* means a child's release from parental care and responsibility. Many parents assume that when their child turns 18 years of age, their responsibility to support and care for that child automatically ends. This assumption is often incorrect.

The criteria governing the age and time at which a child emancipates is governed by each state's individual laws. Although the laws of many states provide that children are emancipated when they turn 18 years of age, not all states provide that a child is emancipated at that age. Even those states that fix age 18 as the date of emancipation provide that under some circumstances a child is still treated as unemancipated for purposes of child support.

In order for a child to be considered emancipated, he or she must have the ability to be self-supporting without requiring further financial support from his or her parents. The ability to be self-supporting requires that the child is able to obtain full-time employment or enroll in college. If a child continues to reside in his or her parent's home and is still a full-time student in high school, even though he or she has reached age 18, the child is not considered able to secure full-time employment or enroll in college until after graduation.

For example, if the child's 18th birthday occurs in January, the child usually cannot graduate from high school until the following June. Many states provide that the noncustodial parent must continue to pay child support until the child graduates from high school or turns 19, whichever occurs first. This practice also means that if the child reaches age 19 before he or she graduates high school, the support obligation terminates at the end of the month in which the child turns age 19, even if the child continues to live with the custodial parent and attend high school past his or her 19th birthday.

Emancipation and AFDC

AFDC rules provide that a custodial parent may continue to receive AFDC if a child is older than 18, a full-time high school student, and will graduate prior to his or her 19th birthday. However, AFDC is not to be paid past the age of 18 for a child who does not expect to graduate from high school until after his or her 19th birthday. In order for a child older than 18 to receive AFDC, the child must be a full-time high-school student. This requirement is intended to encourage children who are receiving AFDC to obtain their diplomas.

Children over 18 can be enrolled in a form of continuing education, in home schooling, or in a home study course instead of a regular high school, and are entitled to receive child support until they reach 19. As long as: 1) the alternative schooling is accredited; 2) the child participates in the schooling program at least 20 hours per week; and 3) the alternative program will produce a high school diploma, the child is considered a full-time high school student for the purposes of child support and/or AFDC.

Children who have dropped out of high school, but return to adult education classes to obtain a GED or similar certificate, are not considered full-time high school students, and support for these children is terminated when they reach age 18.

Unless the support order provides for a prorated child support payment at the end of the obligation, most agencies do not prorate the final payment. Thus, if a child turns 18 on January 7th and is no longer attending high school full-time, the noncustodial parent must make a full payment of child support for the month of January.

A custodial parent whose child will turn 18 before graduation from high school must provide proof of the child's status as a full-time student in order to qualify for support beyond age 18 and until graduation. Normally, a school-provided copy of the child's attendance record that notes the expected date of graduation is sufficient evidence.

Child support and marriage dissolution orders

The CSE agency resolves differences between the state's emancipation laws and the underlying court order in favor of the court order. Some marriage dissolution orders entered before the agency has begun to handle the case differ from the terms normally contained in standard support orders. If the marriage dissolution order contains a clause ordering the noncustodial parent to pay child support until the child reaches 21, the agency enforces this provision, even though the state's emancipation law terminates the obligation at 18. A noncustodial parent who wishes to obtain relief from this additional support burden must petition the court to modify the order.

Many marriage dissolution orders contain special clauses, such as the noncustodial parent pay the child's college costs. Other orders contain provisions for children with special needs that require the noncustodial parent to continue support payments years beyond the legal age of emancipation. Parents whose marriage dissolution orders contain such clauses should discuss them with the agency to clarify the manner in which the agency will enforce these clauses.

Both parents should be certain that the agency is informed of a child's emancipation. We suggest both parents contact the agency about 90 days beforehand to allow the agency enough time to verify the date and implement changes in the billing of the noncustodial parent. Failure to notify the agency that a child has emancipated can cause the agency to overcollect child support from the noncustodial parent and pay extra child support to a custodial parent not entitled to it. Such overpayments cause stressful recoupments of the overpayments from the custodial parent.

Noncustodial parents must remember that the emancipation of their children does not eliminate their legal obligation to pay any child support arrearages that have accrued. All enforcement mechanisms remain in place to collect support arrearages, even though current support is no longer being collected. And interest can continue to be charged on unpaid arrearages until they are paid in full.

Overpayments

We have seen cases in which the noncustodial parent continued to pay child support for more than a year after a child's legal emancipation without either parent's notifying the agency. The typical noncustodial parent informs the CSE agency of the emancipation in order to terminate collection efforts for current child support, but some simply neglect to notify the agency; others do not notify the agency because they do not know of the emancipation; and others assume the agency will automatically terminate collection efforts once the child emancipates.

It is a mistake for a noncustodial parent to assume that his or her current child support obligation will be correctly terminated by the CSE agency. Many agencies rely upon the parents to advise them of the underlying facts that cause the obligation to be terminated. A noncustodial parent should not rely upon the custodial parent or agency to ensure that child support payments are terminated upon the child's emancipation. Every noncustodial parent should know the date his or her child turns age 18, and should contact the agency shortly before the child's birthday to inquire of the child's status past the 18th birthday.

The custodial parent usually has the information the CSE agency needs to determine emancipation, while the noncustodial parent usually has the motivation to cause this review to occur. Unless the noncustodial parent has chosen to have no involvement in the life of his or her child, he or she is usually the best source of inquiries regarding emancipation.

The custodial parent should assume the responsibility to notify the agency of any facts that cause the child to be emancipated. Failure to notify the agency of a child's emancipation does not produce a support windfall for the custodial parent—it simply delays the date of reckoning and inevitably produces an accounting headache resulting from an overpayment by the noncustodial parent.

If overpayment has occurred in a case in which the custodial parent has been receiving AFDC, the CSE agency can easily refund the overpayment to the noncustodial parent, because the child support payment had been retained by government to recoup welfare costs. However, actual repayment to the noncustodial parent can take many months.

If the overpayment has occurred in a nonaid support case, recoupment is more complicated. By the time the agency is notified, it has usually sent the payments to the custodial parent. The custodial parent, who should have known he or she was not entitled to these payments, frequently claims that the overpaid moneys have already been spent. The noncustodial parent is then subject to a long delay in recouping overpayment from the custodial parent.

Some agencies decline to pursue the custodial parent for the over-payment, requiring the noncustodial parent to collect the overpayment by his or her own efforts.

If the CSE agency does take responsibility for recoupment, the agency begins by requesting that the custodial parent voluntarily repay the money. If the custodial parent does not voluntarily repay, the agency might file a civil action to obtain a judgment against him or her, and then enforce this judgment by a wage assignment and other collection measures. Although collecting overpaid child support from a custodial parent is not a pleasant task, it is necessary for the agency to remain neutral in its dealings with both custodial and non-custodial parents.

In addition to overpayments caused by collection of current sup-port beyond a child's age of emancipation, overpayments also occur when a child covered by a support order goes to live with the noncus-todial parent for more than a brief period. When a child covered by a support order lives with the noncustodial parent, the noncustodial parent is no longer obligated to pay child support, unless otherwise specified in the court order.

Most courts give the noncustodial parent credit against his or her support obligation for those periods (other than normal visitation periods) when the noncustodial parent actually supported the child in his or her home. However, unless someone informs the agency of this change of custody, it will continue to enforce the order as issued by the court. The custodial or noncustodial parent should notify the CSE agency of a change in custody, so the agency does not continue to col-lect child support from a noncustodial parent no longer required to pay support.

An overpayment can also occur when the CSE agency fails to stop collection efforts from a noncustodial parent who has completely paid his or her arrearage. Because the agency is required to send a monthly bill to every noncustodial parent showing the total amount owed, the amount currently due, and the amount already paid, the noncustodial parent should be able to track his or her account and notify the agency when the account has been completely paid.

Either through inadvertence, misinformation, or errors, collection efforts sometimes continue beyond the payoff of an arrearages account, and the custodial parent will not normally know that the payment is an overpayment.

When a nonaid custodial parent has been paid support arrearages that exceeded the amount of the noncustodial parent's obligation, the CSE agency usually tries to work with the custodial parent to arrange a repayment schedule.

If the custodial parent who has received an overpayment on arrearages is still entitled to receive current child support, the CSE agency can make an arrangement with the custodial parent to receive a reduced monthly amount in current support to repay the overpayment.

A custodial parent occasionally declines to cooperate in devising a repayment schedule for an overpayment on arrearages, claiming that overpayment was not caused by his or her error. The question is not who is at fault for the overpayment; but rather, who is entitled to the money under the court order. If an error has been made resulting in an overpayment, the noncustodial parent is entitled to be reimbursed.

If a custodial parent declines to cooperate with the agency in arranging a solution to overpayment of an arrearage, the agency is forced to obtain a court order for repayment of the arrearage overpayment. In some situations the agency requires the noncustodial parent to collect the overpayment without governmental involvement.

No matter what solution is found to refund an overpayment to a noncustodial parent, overpayments are troublesome for everyone involved. Rather than subject everyone to the trauma of collecting overpayments from the custodial parent, both parents should inform the CSE agency of any changes that affect collection efforts. Again, parents should immediately report to the agency all changes in custody, emancipation, and payment in full on the account.

Closing a child support case

The CSE agency must first verify the date of emancipation of all of the children in the case. Then the agency must determine whether the noncustodial parent owes any arrearages under the support order. If no arrearages are owed, the agency notifies the noncustodial parent's employer to terminate the wage assignment, removes the noncustodial parent's name from intercept lists, releases any liens on real property, notifies credit bureaus that the account has been paid in full and is being closed, and terminates any other collection or enforcement actions.

With the emancipation of the child and payment in full of all support moneys owed under the child support order, the agency usually sends a letter to the custodial parent advising him or her that the case is paid in full and will be closed. A custodial parent who feels that the case has been closed in error should immediately notify the agency.

The agency might also send to the noncustodial parent a closing letter and a copy of the termination of the wage assignment sent to the employer. The noncustodial parent should be careful to ensure that the employer has received the wage assignment termination notice, as agency staff occasionally fail to send the wage assignment termination notice. The agency might also send a document (such as a satisfaction of judgment, satisfaction of matured installment, or release of lien) verifying that any property liens have been lifted. Unless the agency has recorded a satisfaction of judgment, a satisfaction of matured installment, or a release of lien with the county recorder's office, the noncustodial parent should record the document releasing all liens. The agency or county recorder's office can usually explain the procedures for recording such documents.

Many parents continue to help support their children through college or young adulthood, but parental assistance to an adult child is usually a voluntary act and not a legal obligation. The emancipation of the child means that the child is now an adult and the *legal* obligation of the parents to support him or her has ended.

Chapter 11

Tips to Help You Deal Effectively with a CSE Agency

CSE agencies receive and process thousands of letters and communications every month, most of which come from people who have problems or inquiries that justify a prompt response. Employees make valiant efforts to reply to the letters, calls, and other correspondence they receive, but sometimes the volume of these communications is overwhelming.

Many CSE caseworkers feel that the volume of inquiries they receive prevents them from effectively managing their cases, because they spend so much of their time answering questions and resolving problems. Some caseworkers are responsible for as many as 1,500 child support cases at one time. Although the sheer volume of this work sometimes causes agency workers to feel frustrated, many prioritize their responses to these communications, replying to the most urgent requests first and delaying their responses to less urgent inquiries.

Some parents feel they have been lost in this system. Usually out of frustration, they become angry. In many of these situations, the problems could have been avoided if the parents had known how to deal with the agency. The knowledge you have gained from this book should help you better understand how the process of child support enforcement works and how CSE agencies function. By following the suggestions we have made, you should be able to avoid many problems that commonly plague parents whose lives are impacted by CSE agencies.

Here are some tips for simplifying your child support case.

1. Organize your own records on your child support case

Every custodial and noncustodial parent should keep all of the documents that relate to his or her child support case in one place. Try using a 2" binder (or larger) and folders to separate sections of your records.

2. Record all vital information on your case

Your records should contain the name, address, and telephone number of your CSE agency. Mark your case number clearly on the first sheet of your records—it enables the CSE agency to identify your case. Also record identifying information, such as the name of your caseworker, and information on how to locate and contact the agency by phone.

3. Save all court orders

Make sure you obtain and save a copy of all orders issued by the court pertaining to your case. Many cases have multiple court orders, and some were issued many years ago. Arrange the orders chronologically, with the oldest order on the bottom of the file. This method allows you to easily review the terms of your order, and saves you from having to search through old files looking for a copy. If you are missing a court order, contact the issuing clerk's office to obtain a copy at a reasonable cost.

4. Create a payment history record

You might already have a copy of an audit of your child support case performed by the CSE agency; such audits contain payment history records. If you have no record of the payment history of your case, you can request that the CSE agency send you one. Review the history for accuracy and notify the agency of any errors.

Use the payment history record to begin your own log. Noncustodial parents should record all monthly payments made to the custodial parent and custodial parents should record all monthly payments received.

Since child support cases commonly last for more than 10 years (and some are open from birth until the child emancipates), a payment history log is a useful tool to protect against errors made by the CSE agency or other parent. It will also help you accurately track the progress of your child support case. (See the payment history form on page 175.)

Noncustodial parents should also keep all money order receipts, pay stubs, canceled checks, bank statements, and monthly agency statements showing payments. A word of warning regarding paying child support by money order. Because a money order receipt does not contain the custodial parent's signature that proves that the custodial parent received the money order, and because it is easy to alter a photocopy of a money order receipt, some CSE agencies do not accept photo copies of money orders as proof of payment. A preferred and much safer method of direct child support payment is payment by personal check or by a cashier's check.

5. Create a telephone log

Make a telephone log in which you keep a record of every phone call you make or receive concerning your child support case. (See the telephone log form on page 176.) The log should list the name and phone number of each person with whom you have spoken, the date and time of each telephone call, and any significant information about the contents of the call.

6. Create a correspondence log

Make a copy of every letter you send regarding your child support case. Save every piece of correspondence you receive regarding your case. Arrange this correspondence in chronological order, with the most recent correspondence on the top so you can easily locate any item you may need. This will offer you a complete history of your case.

Telephoning your CSE agency

Patience is a virtue, and when you use a telephone to get information from a CSE agency, patience is a necessity. Most CSE agencies have "telephone trees"—electronic systems for directing callers to the appropriate extension without the use of an operator. Many people find these telephone trees frustrating. Call your CSE agency to request a copy of the agency's "phone tree map," which gives directions on how to best use the telephone tree. By familiarizing yourself with the directions, you can simplify your call and letter ensure that you reach someone who can help you, or you can obtain the information you need directly from the telephone tree.

Caseworkers usually do not answer the telephone to talk with people who call for information about their cases. Because they usually handle hundreds to thousands of cases, many caseworkers are unable to immediately answer questions from a caller. The common practice is to take voice mail messages, determine the answers, and then get back to the inquirers.

Many agencies have personnel employed in the agency's public service units who are trained to answer general questions about the process, but sheer volume sometimes prevents callers from immediately reaching a public service worker or caseworker.

Leaving and receiving telephone messages

If you leave a message, speak slowly and clearly so your message is clearly recorded. State your name, your identifying case number, the reason for your call, and a number where you can be reached during normal business hours. The agency personnel might take as long as a week to return your call—if your inquiry is urgent, you must explain in your message why an immediate answer is needed.

Always be specific in your request. Do not call the agency to check on the general status of your case. When you are specific in your request, the caseworker handling your message can return your call with a precise answer to your specific question(s), such as the status of your case audit, whether a wage assignment has been served on the noncustodial parent's employer, or whether the summons and complaint has yet been served on the noncustodial parent.

If you have voice mail or an answering machine the CSE worker can leave a message for you that answers your questions without ever having to talk with you. If you have not received a return telephone call within one week, you should call the CSE agency again.

Speaking to the caseworker

In order to save time, be prepared for the return call. Make a list of the questions you want to ask the caseworker. Write those questions (and the answers you get in response) in your personal telephone log. This will help you to remember everything you wanted to ask your caseworker, and help prevent multiple telephone calls about the same concern. Good record-keeping will also help the caseworker take appropriate follow-up action to correct any problems.

Even though the process of dealing with a bureaucracy can be frustrating, you should be courteous to CSE caseworkers. Expressions of anger directed at CSE employees rarely help resolve problems and often create complications. Although most of these workers genuinely want to help a courteous parent solve his or her problem, an unpleasant or rude caller can discover that his or her inquiry is relegated to the lowest level of priority. Speak to the caseworker in a reasonable tone of voice using language that motivates him or her to want to help you.

Far too many parents use the opportunity to talk to the caseworker to complain about the quality of service provided by the agency or burden the caseworker with problems regarding the other parent that the caseworker cannot by law handle. For instance, a noncustodial parent might complain that the custodial parent is withholding visitation until the noncustodial parent pays child support. Because visitation and custody issues are not handled by the CSE agency, the CSE agency cannot assist you with visitation and custody disputes. Or, a custodial parent might call complaining that the noncustodial parent is refusing to pay child support until the custodial parent allows visitation, or that the noncustodial parent is harassing the custodial parent. Again, because visitation, custody, and claims of harassment are outside the legal jurisdiction of CSE agencies, the caseworker is not able to advise you on these issues. Complaints such as these utilize valuable time that case workers could have otherwise used to assist parents on a child support-related problems.

This does not mean that you must blindly accept everything you are told by a caseworker. If your call is pertinent to child support issues that are handled by the agency or if an error has been made in your case, clearly express the facts that identify the error, and leave its solution to the caseworker. For instance, if the child has emancipated and the noncustodial parent continues to receive bills from the CSE agency for current support, the noncustodial parent should telephone the agency and leave a detailed message regarding the exact date the child emancipated. Follow up your telephone call with a written letter to the CSE agency and enclose with the letter, any documents that prove your point. Allow time for the CSE agency to receive your letter. Make a follow-up telephone call to the CSE agency only if you haven't heard from the agency since your first call. These steps help ensure that when the caseworker does handle the problem, he or she will already have the information from you by which the billing problem can be resolved.

A parent who feels that the CSE staff is either unable to answer a question or gives an inaccurate answer can request to speak to the caseworker or the caseworker's immediate supervisor to rectify any informational problems. By keeping accurate records of your case, you will be able to provide the proof needed to correct any errors that may occur in the handling of your case.

Generally, CSE agency staff should return your telephone call within one week and should reply to your written correspondence within 30 days. If these time restrictions have not been met, you should make another telephone call and write another letter, to the CSE agency, informing the agency that your call or letter is your second request for a response. If you receive a response from the CSE agency that does not resolve the problem, you should check again with the CSE agency within 30 days to verify that the error has been corrected. For more information on federally mandated response times, please refer to Chapter 3.

Every CSE agency has parents who never seem satisfied with the service or information provided by the agency. Some people often feel that the staff don't respond quickly enough to their inquiries, mishandle their cases, give them inaccurate information, and other similar complaints. If you are a frequent caller, you must remember that each time you call or write the CSE agency, you are taking a CSE caseworker away from working your case or someone else's case. Frequent calls and complaints to caseworkers do not generally improve the quality of service provided by a CSE agency. Refer to pages 172-174 regarding the proper complaint process if you are unhappy with the progress of your case.

Mailing correspondence to the CSE agency

When you do not need an immediate response to your question or inquiry, you should communicate with the agency by mail. Requests for an audit of a child support account, proof of payments made or received, notifications of a change of address or telephone number, change of employment, and other similar information can be effectively communicated by mail.

When you correspond by mail, always include your name and case number. If you fail to list your case number, your letter may be delayed by the process of identifying your case. Send correspondence on regular 8" x 11" business paper. CSE agencies receive too much mail written on torn pieces of paper, less than 4" in size. Small scraps of paper such as these are easily lost in the large volumes of paperwork handled by many agencies.

Your written requests and communications should be specific and to the point—try to address your concerns in a letter no longer than one page. Some parents write voluminous letters to CSE agencies venting anger toward the other parent, the courts, or the agency itself. Some vent about subjects over which the CSE agency has no jurisdiction—such as custody and visitation issues. Excessive writing wastes your time and takes the CSE agency's caseworker away from working your case and the cases of other parents.

It is also helpful if you inform the agency whether or not you need a written response. If your letter simply reports information, requiring the caseworker to respond only delays action. If your letter contains an inquiry that requires a written response, allow the agency about 30 days. If you do not have a reply after 30 days, send a follow-up letter marked "second request," or follow up with a phone call.

Custodial and noncustodial parents should always notify the agency of any change of address, employment, telephone number, or any other significant change that affects the ability of the agency to contact a parent or that might affect the support order. CSE agencies consume too much personnel time trying to locate custodial parents so the agency can send the child support collections, or trying to respond to phone calls or written correspondence, because the parent's address or phone number has changed. Keep the agency updated throughout the duration of your case, because when the custodial parent cannot be located, the agency may close the case.

Some changes in family situations affect the child support obligation or impact the flow of child support collections. A parent should always notify the agency of any change in the custody or emancipation of a child. Custodial parents receiving AFDC should immediately notify the agency when they stop receiving welfare.

Visiting the CSE agency in person

We recommend that every parent who has a child support case being enforced by a CSE agency make every effort to resolve problems by telephone and/or mail before making a personal visit to the office. However, sometimes a parent must personally visit the CSE agency. Agency staff must occasionally conduct a personal interview with a parent or obtain a signature on a document. Sometimes a parent simply feels that a personal visit with a CSE caseworker is necessary to resolve a particular problem.

A personal visit is best made when arranged in advance with an appointment. Having an appointment improves the parent's chances of being able to see a staff member without having to sit for hours in the waiting room, and ensures that the visit will be with the staff member who is most knowledgeable about the case.

If appointments are not available, a parent can choose to drop in to the agency. If a parent comes without an appointment, he or she is usually seen on a first come, first serve basis, but there is usually a lengthy wait. (It is advisable to go early in the day, when fewer other parents are likely to be waiting.) The parent will then be seen by the caseworker assigned to meet with drop-ins on that day. Many parents come to the office each week, and the CSE staff who are available to meet with drop-ins are usually insufficient to see the total number of parents who show up. Many CSE agencies allow drop-ins only on specific days of the week.

Hostile behavior

Personal visits at a CSE agency are sometimes acrimonious. Many people who visit the office have tried to resolve their problems or differences by telephone or mail, and by the time they come to the agency in person, they are frustrated and angry. Although it is often difficult for a parent caught in the emotions of a broken relationship to keep his or her emotions in check when discussing the financial support of the children of that broken relationship, every parent must remember that a hostile outburst will usually cause the CSE agency caseworker to terminate the visit and request that a security officer, usually an armed peace officer, escort the parent out of the building.

While doing so may require great self-control, we recommend that every parent remain outwardly calm when dealing with CSE staff, focus on the facts relevant to the issue that must be resolved, and communicate openly with the worker. Outbursts, crying, threats, and other similar forms of behavior do not usually produce positive results in a CSE agency.

Threats against a CSE worker can result in an immediate response by a law enforcement officer and arrest. Threats against a staff worker are considered serious business and usually cause a criminal investigation. Refrain from making statements that could be interpreted as threats and *never* bring a firearm or other dangerous weapon into a CSE office. Many CSE offices have a full-time sheriff or armed security guard on the premises to arrest those who threaten violence.

Bringing children to the CSE agency

Unless you are unable to make childcare arrangements for your children, do not bring them to the agency. Children do not easily tolerate long delays in waiting rooms, and during personal interviews, they are often disruptive.

If you must bring a child with you, bring items with which your child can occupy him- or herself—games, books, and snacks—to pass the time. You might also bring a friend with you to assist with your children when you are talking with the caseworker.

Preparation for the visit

When you make your appointment, ask the caseworker what papers or records you should bring to the interview—and make sure you bring them. In addition, you should bring your set of personal records and all other paperwork you believe relevant to your inquiry. If the purpose of your visit is to resolve your child support case, you must bring all of the financial information that you haven't already provided to the agency. Bring documentation to support any disagreement you have with the agency's records.

Resolving problems

Information produces results in child support enforcement. A custodial parent should report to the CSE agency pending lawsuits, worker's compensation cases, or any possible inheritances involving the noncustodial parent. The custodial parent should also report to the CSE agency all changes of address, changes in the custodial parent's employment, and changes in the custody of the children.

Keep your file updated and keep track of all payments made to and by you. If the court order requires the noncustodial parent to reimburse one-half of out-of-pocket medical expenses incurred for the child by the custodial parent. Both the custodial and noncustodial parent should keep copies of all medical statements and bills. Custodial parents should maintain copies of unpaid medical statements in order to prove that they are owed reimbursement for medical expenses which they have already paid, but for which they have not yet been reimbursed by the noncustodial parent. Noncustodial parents should keep copies of records to prove they have paid their share of the court-ordered medical costs.

When the CSE agency is working on an action in your case based on information you have provided, request that the agency tell you the estimated time needed for the work to be completed. You should be an active participant in your child support case, but you should also be patient enough to allow the caseworkers to act on the information you have given them.

Perhaps most of the problems that agencies must resolve involve noncustodial parents, because noncustodial parents are the targets of enforcement actions initiated by the agencies. Sometimes even noncustodial parents who pay child support regularly are ensnared by legal remedies meant for nonpayers.

If a noncustodial parent who is complying with a child support order is subjected to enforcement action that appears inappropriate, the parent should remain calm and request that the agency take immediate corrective action. If the noncustodial parent has kept good records, inappropriate enforcement action against a complying parent can usually be corrected quickly and easily.

In requesting corrective action from the CSE agency, the paying noncustodial parent should comply with any legitimate requests for information or documents, request the agency declare an expected resolution date, and follow up to ensure that the agency has taken appropriate action.

A noncustodial parent who has failed to comply with a court order for child support and faces serious legal and financial consequences should not panic. Although paying child support in compliance with a court order is the only acceptable resolution for nonpayment, CSE agencies commonly try to devise payment schedules that enable the noncustodial parent to return to compliance with the court order. Although agencies do not ordinarily compromise the amount owed in child support arrearages, they have considerable flexibility in establishing repayment schedules.

Once a nonpaying noncustodial parent has reached an agreement with the agency, he or she must live up to the agreement. Some noncustodial parents have made promises to CSE agencies in order to convince them to terminate enforcement actions, only to later renege on the agreement. Once a noncustodial parent has gone back on his or her word on an agreement for repayment for past noncompliance with a support order, the CSE agency is not likely to enter into another agreement. The parent will either suffer from severe enforcement actions or must petition the court for relief from the enforcement actions.

If the noncustodial parent later determines that he or she is truly unable to make the payments required by the agreement, he or she should immediately contact the agency to explain the problem and request an opportunity to come to an alternative solution. A noncustodial parent who makes good-faith efforts to work cooperatively with the CSE agency and comply with agreed-upon terms is likely to avoid the severe enforcement actions that the CSE agency has the power to initiate. The noncustodial parent who stops paying child support and is no longer in compliance with a court order, who does not communicate with the agency, who does not offer to agree to an alternative arrangement, and who continuously ignores warnings from the CSE agency stands to suffer serious financial and legal consequences.

The complaint process

A parent who has followed all of the suggestions we have made in this book for resolving problems with a CSE agency, and whose case is being handled in an unsatisfactory manner by the agency, has a legitimate right to complain to a higher authority. CSE agencies and their personnel are not unlike other businesses or governmental agencies: they sometimes make mistakes and the quality of their work may fall below an acceptable level.

While it is not possible to establish a time for each and every function involved in handling a support case, the federal government has established time limits by which all CSE agencies must perform basic services. These time limits cover agency responses to complaints made by telephone or mail. A parent who has made a good faith effort to resolve a problem or dispute with the agency can telephone or write to complain about the lack of action or inappropriate action in the case. A parent who wants to make a complaint about the agency or its workers should be certain to have exhausted all other opportunities to correct the problem and should be certain that his or her concerns are justified.

A complaint should first be directed to the immediate supervisor in charge of the worker or unit handling the case. Most agencies require their employees to handle complaints in an expeditious manner, and most complaints and problems can be resolved by an immediate supervisor. In resolving a complaint about the handling of a case, most supervisors personally review the file to determine whether the agency has handled the problem appropriately.

If the supervisor concludes that the complainant is either wrong or simply does not understand the situation, the supervisor informs the complainant why the complaint is not justified. If the supervisor finds that the case was improperly handled and that the complaint is valid, the supervisor has the power to immediately initiate corrective action.

If your complaint to the supervisor has not produced an acceptable solution, direct your complaint to the person in charge of the complaints. Many CSE agencies have assigned a senior staff member to research and reply to complaints—in some agencies, it is the person in charge of the agency. If the agency has appropriately handled a case under governing laws and regulations, disagreement with child support laws does not establish good cause for a complaint. A parent's unhappiness or disagreement with a decision of a court or agency does not cause the court's or agency's decision to be wrong.

A parent who believes that his or her complaint was not satisfactorily handled by the agency also has the right to bring the complaint to the attention of the county or state agency supervising the child support enforcement program, or to the Office of the Attorney General of the state.

A parent who wants to complain about the handling of his or her case should contact the state's central registry to obtain the name and address of the supervising state agency and the procedures for filing a complaint. If the supervising state agency agrees with the CSE agency's resolution of the complaint, the complainant is advised of that agreement. However, if the state agency determines that the case has not been properly handled, it has the power to direct the CSE agency to take immediate corrective action. Most parental complaints and problems, however, can be resolved by the CSE agency without the intervention of the supervising state agency.

Parents who have the least problems with the enforcement of their child support orders are those who comply with state laws governing child support, and who work within the rules and procedures that CSE agencies must follow. These parents are knowledgeable about the child support enforcement process, and they take seriously their responsibilities to support their children and assist the agency in managing their cases.

Parents who suffer most are those who are not honest with CSE authorities, who constantly try to thwart the system, and who fail to pay or make attempts to avoid paying their legally owed child support.

By becoming an active participant in your own child support case, by keeping good records of your payments and expenses, and by becoming informed about the procedures and laws that regulate child support enforcement agencies, you will avoid many of the problems and pitfalls experienced by parents in the system. Much of the responsibility for making your child support case a smooth and conflict-free experience rests on the shoulders of the parents.

We hope the information we have provided you will help you to better understand and to deal more effectively with the Child Support Enforcement system. It is our hope that understanding this system and its powers will help motivate noncustodial parents to comply with their legal and moral obligations to support their children.

We hope this book will assist more children in receiving the financial support they so desperately need from both of their parents.

We hope that it will help CSE agencies by educating their clientele and freeing them to do the work that society relies on them to do.

We have faith that these goals are not beyond realization.

Payment history

CSE case number_____

Court order number_____

Children_____

Emancipation date or change in custody_____

Monthly support amount_____

Monthly arrears payment_____

Month	Owed	Paid	Balance due
January			
February			
March			
April			
May			
June			
July			
August			
September			
October			
November			
December			

Year_____Total amount owed_____

Telephone log

CSE case number_____

Person called_____

Date_____ Time_____

Contact made   Yes   No

Message left   Yes   No   Return call requested_____

Reason for telephone call_____

_____

_____

_____

Return call received on_____ Time_____

Results obtained_____

_____

_____

_____

Action to be taken by CSE agency_____

_____

Action to be taken by parent_____

_____

Follow up on_____

_____

Glossary

This glossary is written in common, everyday language for non-attorneys. It is not meant to be a legal dictionary for lawyers.

Absent parent. The parent (either the father or mother) who is physically absent from the home and who does not have custody of the minor child. He or she is legally responsible to assist in supporting the child. Usually called the noncustodial parent.

Accrue. To build up or increase.

Adjudication. A judgment or decree by a court or administrative officer.

AFDC (Aid to Families with Dependent Children). A welfare cash grant issued to a family with children that needs financial assistance, usually because the head of the household (the custodial parent) is unemployed and not receiving child support or childcare assistance from the noncustodial parent.

Administrative officer. An appointed official who presides over child support cases instead of a judge or commissioner.

Affidavit. A written declaration or statement made under oath and under penalty of perjury.

Allegation. An assertion or claim.

Answer. A written legal response filed with a court by a defendant in response to a civil complaint filed against him or her.

Arrearage/arrears. Unpaid child or spousal support that has built up under a court order.

Assignment. The surrender by an AFDC recipient of all rights to support arrearages owed the recipient, and of the right to receive current child support, as the result of the receipt of AFDC.

Bankruptcy. A legal proceeding in which a person who is financially insolvent requests the federal bankruptcy court to determine his or her debts and use his or her assets to pay those debts. Property in bankruptcy usually is administered for the benefit of the bankrupt person's creditors. Some forms of bankruptcy seek to discharge all debt if there are no assets to distribute to the creditors. Child support obligations cannot be discharged by bankruptcy.

Bench warrant. An order issued by a court for the arrest of a person who has failed to appear in court as ordered. Can also be issued for a witness who has failed to appear in response to a subpoena.

Blood test. Process by which the claimed father, mother, and child have blood drawn and tested to determine whether the man is the biological father of the child. The blood samples are sent to a laboratory for genetic HLA or DNA testing to determine parentage.

Complaint. A document filed with a court that initiates a civil legal action. (Also known as a petition.)

Contempt. Willful disobedience of or disrespect for a court, judge, or legislative body.

Cross reference case. A separate case involving one parent in common, but in which there are other children by a different father or mother. Either the custodial parent or the noncustodial parent can have cross reference cases.

Custodial parent/person. The person with whom the child resides. This person is not necessarily a parent, but can be a relative or other guardian. This person is responsible for maintaining a home for the child.

Default. Failure by a defendant in a civil action to file a written response with the court as required by law after having been served with a summons and complaint or petition.

Defendant. The person who is being sued for parentage and/or child support.

Direct payment. Child support or spousal support paid directly to the custodial parent by the noncustodial parent.

Disregard. The first $50 received in child support each month which was formerly paid to an AFDC custodial parent in addition to the welfare grant as an incentive to a welfare recipient to cooperate with CSE agencies. Disregard payments were generally eliminated by the Welfare Reform Act of 1996.

Docket number. The number assigned by a court to a civil or criminal case. It identifies the court action and is used on all documents filed with the court in that case.

Emancipated. The legal age at which a child is considered to be released from parental responsibility and is considered an adult.

File. To deliver a document to the clerk of a court to be included in the official records of a case.

Foreign order. A court order issued by another county, state, or nation, outside of the jurisdiction in which the custodial parent resides.

Garnishment. A process by which, under a court order, money or property owed to a judgment debtor is taken from a third person to satisfy the debt (also known as a wage assignment).

Good cause. A standard by which a welfare recipient is excused from cooperating with the CSE agency, because cooperation would endanger the welfare recipient or the children. A good cause finding usually requires documentation of a history of violence and abuse by the noncustodial parent toward the welfare recipient.

Hardship. A condition which causes a financial strain on the ability of a parent to support his or her children.

Health insurance order. A court order that requires a noncustodial parent to obtain health and dental insurance for the children and to add them to the policy.

Income and Expense Declaration. A form completed by a parent under oath, describing that parent's income, assets, expenses, and liabilities. Used to help determine the correct amount of child support to be paid by the noncustodial parent.

Intact family. A family in which both parents reside together with the children.

Intercept. A process by which CSE agencies take a certain percentage of a noncustodial parent's unemployment insurance payments, disability insurance payments, income tax returns, and lottery winnings to pay child support arrearages owed by the noncustodial parent.

Judgment. A written order by a judge, referee, or administrative officer determining parentage of and support for a child.

Jurisdiction. Legal authority of a court over a person, geographical area, or case.

Lien. An encumbrance placed upon property owned by a judgment debtor which prevents the sale, transfer of title, or refinancing of the property until the debt is paid.

Long-arm. The means by which a court can obtain jurisdiction over an individual who resides outside the jurisdiction in which the court is located.

Mediation. A process in which a third person assists disputing parties to resolve or settle their differences.

Medicaid. Funded by the Social Security Act's Title XIX Federal Medical Assistance Program (Medicaid), this program is administered by the Department of Health Services. The federal government provides matching funds to state agencies that are responsible for providing health and medical care to adults and children who meet the eligibility standards. Recipients of AFDC or Supplemental Security Income/State Supplemental Payment (SSI/SSP) are automatically eligible to receive medical benefits under this program. Some individuals who receive a form of AFDC or SSI/SSP, but who do not receive cash assistance, can still be eligible to receive medical benefits.

Military allotment. A deduction for child support from the salary of a noncustodial parent on active duty in the United States military.

Minute order. Official record of a court proceeding prepared by the court clerk. A minute order is not a judgment.

Modification. An order changing the terms of another court order.

Motion. An application made to a court or judge to obtain a judicial ruling.

Noncustodial parent. The parent (either the father or mother) who is physically absent from the home and does not have custody of the minor child. He or she is legally responsible to assist in supporting the child. Also called the absent parent.

Obligee. The person to whom money or other property is owed by a judgment or a contract.

Obligor. The person who owes money or other property as a result of a judgment or a contract.

Order after hearing. Written order signed by a judge after a hearing.

Order of examination. A court proceeding in which a judgment debtor is questioned under oath about his or her assets.

Order to show cause. A court order requiring a party to a civil action (either parent) to appear in court on a specific date and time to explain why the court should not take a particular action in the case.

Pass-on. Child support collections paid to an AFDC recipient because they exceed the AFDC cash grant paid to the recipient. Also know as "excess."

Paternity. The establishment of a legal biological relationship of father and child.

Petition. A document filed with a court that initiates a civil legal action. Also known as a complaint.

Plaintiff. The person who files a civil lawsuit to begin legal action against another person.

Quash. To vacate or make void.

Reciprocity. The process of cooperation between states and countries to establish and enforce child support orders by recognizing and enforcing the laws and court orders of each jurisdiction.

Reimbursement. An amount fixed in a judgment ordering the defendant to repay the government for welfare paid by the government on behalf of a child.

Stipulation. An agreement (usually reduced to writing and filed with the court) between the parties to a civil lawsuit.

Service of process. The procedure by which a party to a civil action delivers legal papers (writs, summons, etc.) to the opposing party.

Set aside. To cancel, annul, or revoke a prior judgment of a court.

Subpoena. A court order that requires a person to appear to testify in court.

Summons. A court order directing a person to respond to or answer a civil complaint.

Tax intercept. The process by which a child support judgment debtor's federal and state income tax refunds are diverted to pay a support arrearage.

Transitional childcare. A welfare program by which welfare recipients who stop receiving AFDC due to employment, but who can't afford to pay childcare costs, receive subsidized childcare assistance, usually for one year.

UIFSA Uniform Interstate Family Support Act. (See URESA.)

URESA (Uniform Reciprocal Enforcement of Support Act). The statute which enables one state to request assistance from another state in establishing or enforcing a child support order against a parent located in the other state.

Visitation credit. A percentage applied to a child support calculation to reflect the amount of time a child lives with the noncustodial parent.

Wage assignment. A court order requiring the employer of a noncustodial parent to deduct an amount for child support from the wages of the noncustodial parent (also known as a garnishment).

Welfare Reform Act. The popular title of the Personal Responsibility and Work Opportunity Reconciliation Act of 1996.

Writ of execution. A court order authorizing the seizure of an asset (bank account, etc.) of a noncustodial parent who owes past due child support. The order usually authorizes the seizure of assets up to the total amount of past due child support owed under the judgment. (Also known as a levy.)

About the authors

Bonnie White, a mother of two children, has worked as a child support enforcement officer for the Family Support Division of the Office of the District Attorney of Contra Costa County, California, for six years. She is responsible for establishing and enforcing paternity and child support orders. Bonnie has tracked down hundreds of missing noncustodial parents and served them with legal actions; she has obtained countless default judgments against unresponsive noncustodial parents; she has audited thousands of accounts; she has assisted in welfare fraud investigations; she has utilized nearly every enforcement action in this book; and she has assisted many custodial and noncustodial parents in resolving problems with their child support cases.

Douglas Pipes has been a deputy district attorney in Contra Costa County, California, for 24 years, five of which he served as the senior deputy in charge of the Family Support Division. A graduate of Harvard Law School and a member of the California Bar since 1969, Doug has written and sponsored many of California's most effective child support laws, including the State Licensing Match System (SLMS), the California statute requiring the California Department of Motor Vehicles to collect Social Security numbers of driver's license applicants; and the California Early Match Employment Program (New Employment Registry System—NERS). In 1993 Doug received the highest award given by the California Family Support Council, the Truly B. Knox Award, for outstanding contribution to the child support enforcement program.

Bonnie and Doug know firsthand the problems experienced by parents who deal with Child Support Enforcement Agencies, and have published this book to help parents understand how this system works and the laws that control the process. We believe that parents who understand the workings of the system are best able to avoid the frustrations it can cause. Empowered with the knowledge of the system, a parent can help ensure that it protects the well-being of every child for whom it was created, while treating both of the parents of that child with dignity and fairness.

Index

Foster care, 33-34
Fraud, welfare, 37-39, 56

Garnishment, wage, 94-99
Good cause, 28-29
Guidelines, child support, 82-91

Hardship deductions, 88-89
Health insurance support, 49-51
High school students,
   supporting, 154-155
Hostile behavior, at the CSE
   agency, 169-170

Informal modifications of support
   orders, 47-48
Information, supplying, 45-46
Insurance
   benefits, 89-90
   support, 49-51
Intact families, 77-78
Interest, 106-110
Internal Revenue Service
   (IRS), 99-100, 112
International Reciprocity
   Directory, 148-151
International support
   enforcement, 137-139
Interstate actions, 125-139
IV-D agencies, 20, 141
IV-D cases, 72

Judgments, default, 78-81

Live-in noncustodial parents, 38
Long Arm Service, 68
"Long arm" statutes, 129-131

Management, case, 93-116

Marriage dissolution orders, 156
Medi-Cal, 30, 34-35, 77
Medicaid, 30, 34-35, 77
Medical support
   enforcement, 49-51
Minor-mothers, 35-36
Minors, summons and
   complaints for, 69
Missing parent, locating, 53-63
Modification, of interstate
   orders, 135-137
Modification review, 121-124
Money orders, payment by, 164
Motion for Intervention, 95

*National Directory of New
   Hires,* 61
National Reference Center—
   Administration for Children
   and Families, 21
Nonaid cases, 41-52, 124
Nonaid vs. AFDC cases, 85
Noncustodial parent
   case opened by, 48-49
   locating in existing case, 61-63
   locating in new case, 57-61
   self-employed, 87-88, 98
Notice of Assignment, 95

Office of Child Support
   Enforcement (OCSE), 82,
   100-101
Office of Juvenile Justice and
   Delinquency Prevention, 56
Office of the Judge Advocate
   General, 81
Overpayments, after
   emancipation, 156-159